For my husband, Craig, who knew I could do it.

Thanks, Baby!

Party Central

By Mandy Lawson

Copyright @ 2009

No part of this book may be reproduced or transmitted in any form or by means, graphic, electronic, or mechanical, including photocopying, recording, taping, or by any information storage retrieval system, without the permission in writing, from the author.

Chapter 1

My name is Lora Kate London, but everyone calls me L.K. I am currently in a state of chaos. My roommate, Kendra, has just announced that she has met her "soul mate" on the Internet, of all places, and she is moving to Africa with him so they can live on their love. What Bull! That leaves me with a two-bedroom apartment in Manhattan! Do you know how much rent is for a two-bedroom apartment? In Manhattan? Imagine paying for a small country and you will know my pain. I don't know what I'm going to do. I just got fired. Again. It wasn't really fair. I didn't mean to spill (throw) coffee on that "nice" man, who by the way was my ex-boyfriend who cheated on me with a stripper. That's my life, and now I have to find a new job and a new roommate. This is great. Just great.

I wake up with the only motivation that can wake me up: Coffee! I stretch my long legs and run my fingers through my honey blonde hair that is sticky with yesterday's gel. Yikes! I saunter into the kitchen and press the button to awaken my coffeemaker, but nothing happens. I try again. It must be broken. I need my coffee. I can't think or move without my coffee.

My thoughts are only motivated by the dream of getting coffee. I can't go across the street to Java's. They fired me yesterday. I'll have to go to Starbucks. I hate Starbucks. They're always busy and that lady on the front of all the cups creeps me out. I'll have to deal. I must have the coffee.

As I enter my bathroom, which is the best part of the apartment because it has the big, whirlpool style bathtub made of purple marble (who knew, right?); I noticed that when I switched the light on, it didn't do anything. What is going on? First my coffee maker died and now my light doesn't work. I change the bulb and try again. Nothing. Crap. Now I have to get ready in the dark.

I put on the jeans that I wore yesterday, along with a T-shirt that says, "My cell phone loves me." I took the elevator only because I love to sit on the bench that is covered with red velvet. What? I know what you're thinking? I'm not a geek. I only like the bench. Maybe I'll buy one. Okay, so I am a geek.

I move quickly past Java's and walk straight into Starbucks shielding my sea green eyes (Today's new contact color; my eyes are really hazel) from the creepy girl on the sign. I order a double tall cappuccino and wait. This is torture. No one should have to wait this long for coffee. I finally get my order and kindly tell the waiter that I wouldn't be here if I didn't have to give my coffee maker a funeral. He looks at me and smiles. Maybe I should apply here. NO! I will not give in to the creepy Starbucks girl. That's what she wants me to do.

I walk back to my apartment and check my mail. I take the stack upstairs and unlock the door. I flip the switch and nothing happens. What is going on? Is the whole building without power? Weird. I drink my coffee in the dark and squint as I attempt to read my mail. As I open my electric bill, I notice a bright, pink slip fall to the ground. Festive. I reach down, pick up the bill, and it all comes to me. I forgot to pay my bill. They (I have no idea who. Maybe aliens.) have shut off my power. I guess I should have known that this would happen. I don't have a job, which means no money. No money means

I can't pay my bills. I may have to move back in with my parents. Oh, no, I have to get a job today.

As I finish my coffee, I sit on my balcony and read the want ads. I want a real job. A cool job. A job that won't embarrass my mother. Let's see. Truck driver (eww), waitress (um, no), retail (maybe), cosmetics (hmm...), professional video game player (what? They have those?), nanny (yeah, right), party planner (I can do that. I like parties).

After deciding my destiny, I reach for my cell phone, dial the number listed, and wait in anticipation. Someone comes on the line, "Hello. Party Central."

"Hi. I'm Lora Kate London and I am calling about your ad for a party planner."

"Do you have any experience?" asks the mysterious person on the other end.

"Um... I have thrown many parties in my life. So, yes. I have experience," I say. I'm only stretching the truth a little.

"Can you come in at 3:30 p.m. today?"

I say, "Yes! I'll be there. Thank you." She hung up. Yes! Possible income. Now, what does a party planner wear? Heels?

Definitely. Suit? No. Cute, little black dress? Oh, yeah! I took a shower in the dark and went to the lobby bathroom to curl my hair. I still have some time before the interview. What can I do in the dark?

I decide to find lunch. I search through my dark refrigerator and find nothing. I finally settle on a can of Spaghetti O's and then I remember I can't warm them up. Oh well, I eat them anyway. I still have plenty of time so I call Sam Bridges, my nearest and dearest friend in the Big Apple. He is a local weatherman here in New York. He's kind of like those crazy weather channel men who go out in the hurricanes to see if the wind is really blowing, but instead he goes out in the snow to show us that it's really snowing. Weather people crack me up. He picks up the phone after the 50th ring.

"What?" he groans.

"Sam, I think I have found a job."

"What kind of job? Another waitressing job?" he says sleepily.

"Are you asleep? And no, it's not another dead end job. I'm going to be a party planner," I say with pride.

"Are you kidding? You know you have a black record. They are not going to hire you, and yes, I'm asleep. I worked last night, unlike some people," he says.

"That is not fair. They will hire me. You just wait. I bet I get it. I'm a people person."

"I bet that you don't. If you get that job, I'll pay for your electricity to be turned back on," he says in a haughty voice.

"How did you know my electricity was turned off? I just found out today," I ask.

"L.K., it's been turned off for a week. I came over to get my DVDs and you had no electricity. You really have to pay attention and stop staying at your parents' house."

"I only stayed over there for a week. Mom and Dad are in Barbados and I had to watch the fish," I say in defense.

"You stayed over there to eat their food!" he says.

"Oh well. I've gotta go. My interview is in an hour. You coming over tonight?" I ask.

"Sure, if you get your electricity turned back on."

"Gee, thanks for the confidence."

"If you get your job and I pay for your lights, we are not watching *Signs* again. I hate that movie. It's so cheesy. There is no way that Mel Gibson can be a lethal weapon and a priest. It's just not feasible. What's that do for your confidence?" he adds.

"Whatever. Bye." I hung up. How dare he bash *Signs*. M. Night is a genius. We will be watching it. I get dressed and lock my door. I'm off to land me a job.

I take the elevator again only to find another person. He is very tall and he is sitting on my bench. Would it be awkward to sit beside him? Maybe I should ask him to move. No, that would be weird. How do you explain to a person that you claim the elevator bench as yours? You can't. I'll stand. It seems like hours before the doors trap us inside. The muzak is annoying and weird. The man seems nervous about something. Maybe he didn't pay his bill either.

The doors part as if Moses were standing in front of us. I gave the lurch a little finger wave and head out into the beautiful city. I love New York. It has a certain crazy atmosphere that I love. Then again, it could be the smog. Who knows?

I find the party agency, Party Central Co. How original. I gracefully walk to the office upstairs. Why is it that all of the offices are upstairs? It's like they want you to work for it. After walking up two flights, I begin to wonder what sorts of things are downstairs.

Are they filled with reception halls, storage rooms, aliens? Hmmm…just a thought. I enter the office with pride and confidence. I better get this job. I would really love to stop living in the dark ages.

"Hello. You must be Laura Kane," says the woman behind the small desk.

"Actually, I'm Lora Kate. You can call me L.K. Who am I meeting with today?" I ask.

"Mr. Sparks will see you in a moment. Please have a seat, L.K. My name is Margaret and you can call me Marge," she says.

I take a seat and wonder about Marge. I wonder what her history is. Where did she come from? She sounds like she lives in Brooklyn. She has fire red hair and matching lipstick. She is wearing a skin tight leopard print top over some black spandex pants. She looks like she knows how to have fun. I wonder what Mr. Sparks is like. I bet he's a short, stumpy man with no life. I probably will get a job making coffee and running errands. I don't want to make coffee anymore.

Her voice jolts my thoughts. "Mr. Sparks will see you now," Marge says. I walk through the hall way lined with Thomas Kinkade paintings. I enter through the oak door and stop in my tracks. Dude is hot! Mr. Sparks is definitely not a short, stumpy man. I am going to get this job. I have mad flirting skills.

"Hello, Mr. Sparks. I'm Lora Kate London, but you can call me L.K. I'm here to interview for a party planner position," I say in my sexiest voice.

"Ah, yes, Ms. London. Please take a seat," he says. His blonde hair went perfect with his tan body. His eyes are an ocean blue color. Oh, man, I need this job. "I'm going to get straight to the point. I'm in quite a hurry today. I need a party planner right away. I have many parties coming up and my last planner had to take a sabbatical for mental health reasons. My assistant said that you have experience, right?"

"Right. I have planned many parties. I can start any time."

"Great. I see on your resume that you graduated from NYU with a degree in Oral Communications/Drama. I also see a long list of coffee houses that you were fired from. What happened there?" he asks.

"Um...I only got fired from those places because my managers just didn't understand me. I can't serve my ex-boyfriends hot coffee. I get the urge to dump coffee on them and I can't help myself. Ok, now I'm babbling. Sorry," I say. Crap, now I've shared my lovely job history and I can't work for the cute guy.

"Well, I can understand that. Here is a binder full of information about my company and how I like things to go. Everything you need to know is in this binder. Take it home, study it, memorize it, and come back tomorrow morning at 9:00 a.m. ready to work. Wear comfortable clothes, you'll be working in the office tomorrow on the phone. I'll give you some advance pay in the morning. Give Marge all of your information. Great to have you on board," he says. Was that it? Did I just get hired? Talks fast that one.

I give him a huge hug and then back away quickly and apologize. I was so happy and excited that I got carried away. I backed out of his office quickly before he could change his mind. I gave Marge all of my information; Driver's license and such. I need to run home, since I'm wearing my Jimmy Choos…there will be no running. I walk home to call Sam. He owes me. Big.

I walk into my apartment and call Sam on my cell. "Sam, I got the job even with my black record and I start tomorrow. You better stop by the electric company on the way over and bring pizza. I feel like pepperoni and cheesy bread."

"You're kidding. I figured you would be crying by now. I already paid your bill and I bought cake," he says.

"Aww, Sam, you're so nice to have no confidence in me. Bring the pizza and we're watching Signs! Bye." I hung up and switched the lights on. The illuminated room made me feel bubbly. Advance pay! Yes! Electricity! I turn on the radio began to sing a little Britney Spears while I made a huge batch of coffee. No funeral for you Mr. coffee maker.

Chapter 2

I buzz Sam up as soon as he arrives. He walks into my apartment with his arms full of goodies. The first thing I see is the cake. It's the birthday kind with the sugary, white icing and pretty, colored roses on top. "It's not my birthday," I say. "And it says Happy Birthday, Bapi." Sorry Bapi, but I'm eating your cake.

"I know, but it was the only one they had. It was a mess up. Hey, I could use some help here," he says as he struggles with the cake, pizza, movies, and a mysterious green bag.

"What's in the bag?" I ask.

"You'll see," he says in a curious tone. I wonder what is in there. Sam has never bought me a gift except for birthdays and Christmas. Maybe it's a good luck present.

"Okay, here is the itinerary for the night: First, we watch Signs because I love it. We also eat the pizza and cheesy bread. Next, we watch Mars Attacks! because it's weird and funny. Then, we eat cake. How does that sound?" I ask.

Sam says, "How about you open this first." He hands me the green bag. I pull out all of the white tissue paper and reach in to find a little red box. I look at him with his wild sandy hair falling over his hazel eyes looking straight at me. How strange. This feels really odd. The only things I know that come in little red boxes are rings with commitments attached to them. I slowly open the red box and find a bottle cap. On the back of the cap holds an engraving, "To an unlikely match." I look at Sam and back at the cap. What is he trying to ask me? We are just friends. We have been through too much to ruin our friendship. What do I say? Should I say thanks? I don't know what to do. It's a bottle cap, what am I supposed to say? Words. I need words. Any words will do, L.K. "Umm…"

"Don't you remember that cap? I met you five years ago today. You were a freshman at NYU and I was a sophomore. We were taking a summer class and you ran into me in the hallway and called me a big jerk. Then you proceeded to continue your rant by telling me that I should watch where I was going and learn to move out of the way. You handed me your bottled coke and you hit me on the shoulder and told me to stop giving you the Starbucks look. I gave you my number and told you to meet me at Starbucks at 5:00 p.m. Then,"

I interrupt, "I stood you up and called you to say I couldn't meet there because I hate the Starbucks girl. Oh, my gosh! I can't believe you remember the day that we first met. That is unbelievable."

He says, "An unlikely match would be our friendship. Most people do not become friends that way."

"Don't get all mushy. I can't believe you remember the exact day. Sam, you're a big softy. Okay, so…let's watch Signs to celebrate my new job," I say as I stuck the cap in my pocket.

"Tell me about this new job," Sam says.

"Well, it is all kind of weird. I walk into Mr. Sparks' office and he repeated my bad work history and then he gave me the job. Weird, huh? He was really nice and hot. I think I see love in the forecast."

"I'm sure you do. It's kind of strange that he just gave you the job without a real interview. He probably just hired you because of your looks.

"Gee, thanks, Sam. I thought it was because of my confident and cheery personality. You have no faith in me at all. You have officially insulted me. Just turn on the movie."

We sat in silence as the movie played. I couldn't concentrate. What if I did just get the job because I'm pretty? Oh well. He's cute. I'm cute. We make a perfect match. I glance over to Sam who is surprisingly looking right at me. "What?"

"You are not watching the movie. I'm sorry. I shouldn't have said that. I'm sure you got the job because of your personality and your excitement," he says.

"You're forgiven, I guess. It does seem kind of weird that I got the job without any real experience and I did wear the little black dress and Jimmy Choos. Can we start the movie over? I want to watch it from the beginning."

"Fine, but you have to agree to watch *Die Hard* instead of *Mars Attacks!* I can't watch that movie again. It's weird and stupid."

"I know. That's why I like it." He gives me a look so I say,

"Fine. We will watch *Die Hard*."

"Yes!" he exclaims in a perfect Napoleon Dynamite voice.

We finished *Signs* and *Die Hard* along with the pizza and cake. Sam fell asleep and I covered him with my quilt and pattered softly to my bedroom. I have a long night ahead of me. I have to read that binder cover to cover and memorize the beautiful contents that lie inside.

I change into my teal nightie and crawl into bed. I'm 23 years old and I'm single, so this job is going to be awesome. I hope there is some sort of travel involved. I read through every page with excitement. I get to organize every party. I will be the one who orders everything and sets it all up. I even get to attend the events. I hope there will be celebrity parties to plan. I glance over to my clock. 1:00 a.m. I better get some sleep. I set my alarm and finally start my

REM cycle when I hear a loud bang. "What was that?" I run to the living room and find Sam still asleep on the couch. I shake him.

"What?" he asked in a groggy voice.

"Did you hear that? That loud bang?"

"No. What do you think it was?"

"I don't know, but it woke me up. I think it came from downstairs. Should we go check it out?"

"Sure, but you might want to get a robe or something," he says as he shields his hazel eyes. I look down and notice that my nightie took a trip south and my boob was hanging out. "Crap!" I cover myself and run to the bathroom. Sam is laughing hysterically. I am so embarrassed. Only me. This would only happen to me. I change into shorts and a tank top. Great! I knew I should have put on my robe before I woke him up. I didn't think. Stupid, stupid!

Sam and I run downstairs to find police cars everywhere. "What is going on?" I ask the short, plump officer.

"Accident. Krispy Kreme truck plowed right into the side of the building," he says.

"Oh, is the driver okay?" Sam asks.

"Yeah, he fell asleep at the wheel. He's fine. Just shaken up a bit. You folks can go back to sleep," he says as he walks out to the truck. With all of the police cars around you would think something serious happened. Now we all know they only came to raid the donut truck. Figures.

Sam and I walk back upstairs. Old Mrs.Tragger stopped us in the hall and says, "What's all the commotion about? I'm trying to get my beauty sleep."

"Oh, nothing. The police found a donut truck," I say.

"Hmph…hey we still on for BINGO Saturday night?" she asks.

"Yep. Just you, me, and the BINGO boards," I say with a smile. I play BINGO with her once a month and she cooks me one hot meal a week. She needs a BINGO partner and I need to eat. "Goodnight Hildie."

"Don't you call me that. I hate that name. I should have never told you my first name. You call me May or don't call me," her voice disappeared behind her door. I unlock my door and trip on my rug. My feet fly above my head and I land with a thud. Sam lifts me off the ground and throws me on my bed. "Goodnight, Klutz Queen," he says.

"Hey! Where are you going?" I ask.

"Home," he answers.

"Why? It's almost 2:00 a.m. You might as well stay here."

"I guess, but once you get a new roommate, I'm staying at home from now on. There are no monsters in your closets and Mrs. Tragger is scary enough to frighten any criminal."

"Fine," I say. "Goodnight.

Chapter 3

I awoke to the smell of bacon and coffee. I glance at my clock. 6:00 a.m. Early. Too early. Oh, wait! I have a job now and I have to get up early. I walk into the kitchen and Sam hands me a cup of Joe. I smell the brew and sit at the table. "Thanks."

"I thought I would make you breakfast on your first day," Sam says.

"Awww. Thanks Mom, but I'm a big girl. I won't cry at Kindergarten. I promise," I say in a sarcastic tone.

He hands me a plate of bacon, eggs, and wheat toast. I make a sandwich with it all and look at Sam. "Hey, thanks for breakfast, Sammy."

"You're welcome. I've gotta run. I have to be in the newsroom ready to air at 8:00 a.m. Good luck today and call me at lunch." He grabs his keys and walks out the door. Sam is not really crazy like the weather channel people. I only say that to torture him. He graduated from NYU with a degree in meteorology. He is the funniest weatherman I know. Well, he's the only weatherman I know, but I bet he is the funniest.

I finish breakfast and get dressed. I love that I can dress comfy for this job. I flat iron my hair and get dressed in jeans and a pink Ralph Lauren polo. I look in my closet and decide to wear Birkenstocks. They are the most comfortable shoes in the whole world. I grab my bag and walk out the door.

As I walk down the street, a nervous feeling overwhelms me. What if I'm not good at this job? What if I suck and totally screw everything up? What if my outfit is too casual? I really need this job. Well, I really need the money. I'll have to do my best. I climb the stairs at Party Central Co. and reach the office. There has to be an elevator somewhere. The climbing is killing me. Marge is already at her desk talking away on the phone in her cheetah print today. She really likes those animal prints. She nods at me to say hello and I wave at her as I walk down to Mr. Sparks' office.

I open the door and hear a yelp. The door smacked him right in the nose and flattened him out on the floor. Crap! His nose is bleeding! I reach for a Kleenex on his desk and reach down to help him. Crap! I have jacked up his face! I'm fired. I just know it. I might as well kiss this job goodbye. He waves his hand at me that he needs no help. He rises and takes the tissue.

"So, Ms. London, you sure know how to make an entrance," he says as he holds a tissue to his nose.

"I am so sorry. I had no idea you were behind the door," I apologize.

"It's okay. I'm fine. Let me show you to your office," he says as he walks. I still have a job. Yeah, me!

"I get an office. How cool! I mean, that's nice," I say. I tried not to sound so excited, but my own office! As Napoleon Dynamite would day, "That's flippin' sweet!" I walk into the office with a huge

24

window that displays the entire city! A view! I love New York City and I love this job!

"Ms. London, here is the contact information. Your first task is to plan a birthday party. She is sixteen year old who wants an Egyptian themed party. You have a Rolodex on your desk. Call her parents first to get an idea of a budget and take it from there. Every number that you need is on your desk. 12:30 p.m. is lunch. You can go home at 5:00 p.m. If you need anything, Marge's extension is 002 and my office, cell, and home numbers are listed also. Your mailbox is in the lounge. Your check should be in there before lunch. You may decorate your office anyway you like within reason. Remember sometimes you meet clients in here so decorate professionally. Use the petty cash in your safe to pay for lunch and anything else you need for your office. Marge does not buy supplies. You'll have to get them yourself. She says she is not paid to deliver only to answer the phone. Have a good day," he says as he walks out. That fine man and his fast talking is giving me butterflies.

Wow! I have a lot to do. I start by calling the parents. I found out her name is Micayla Jenson. Her parents let me know that there is no budget. Awesome! They just want their "Micayla Bug" to be happy. I am psyched. I picked out ten places to call for party supplies. Micayla wants a famous band, animals, and everything else. She wants her party to be unforgettable. I tried to think of what kind of band would be good for an Egyptian themed party and I decided that I would try The Plain White Tees, Switchfoot, and Fallout Boy. (None of which go with the theme) I am nervous. I have never talked with anyone famous before. I dial the number and a woman answers. "Hello. May I direct your call?"

"Yes, this is Party Central. May I speak with The Plain White Tees' manager?" I say in my most professional voice.

"One moment please," she says and the line switches. That was easy. "Hello," a man's voice answers.

"Yes, this is Party Central and I would like to see if I can schedule The Plain White Tees for a performance?" I ask.

"For when?" he asks.

"In two weeks on Saturday July 8th."

"Nope, can't happen. They are booked for three months. Sorry." And the line went dead. Crap!

I then tried Switchfoot. Different people. Same answer. Two weeks is too short a notice. Oh Snap! This is not going well. I need coffee. I went across the hall into the lounge. Coffee was brewing and Marge was propped against the counter. "Hey Doll," she says. "How's your first day?"

"It's okay. I can't find a band available for this girl's party. I'm starting to get worried. I don't want her to be disappointed," I say as I grab a cup.

"Honey, you gotta be tough. Tell 'em you won't take no for an answer. Tell 'em that you don't care how much it costs. Give 'em a competition name. Tell 'em Diddy said he would do the gig for less. Don't let them stomp on you. Go get 'em girl!"

Her motivation speech made me run back to my office. I am ready! I am hot! No one hangs up on Lora Kate London. I grab the receiver and punch in the number for The Plain White Tees again. I demanded to speak with someone. "Hello." It's the same guy again. Oh no. NO! Do not get scared. Do not wimp out! Keep up the rage!

"This is Party Central Co. again. I would like The Plain White Tees in two weeks. Either you move something around or I'll call Diddy back and give him the gig," I say with authority.

"Well..." he says.

"Well nothing! We pay a lot more than anyone you have."

"Well, I don't want Diddy getting all the fame. He has already changed his name a hundred times. I'll see what I can do. Give me your number," he says. I gave him my number and laid the receiver down. Yes! Yes! Yes! I am woman! Hear me roar! I am on fire!

I spent the next three hours ordering and scheduling. I ordered two black panthers and many tall, pointy-eared dogs. I've ordered Pyramids, Sphinxes, and everything under the sun except King Tut's tomb. (That would be cool, though) I scheduled Egyptian dancers. I didn't even know they had those. I also ordered invitations that fit inside little glass pyramids.

I noticed that it was 12:35 p.m. I called Sam and told him to meet me at Pete's Pizza. I grabbed my bag and walked downstairs. I think I'm going to like this job. It's fun and my boss is HAWT!

I walk into Pete's with a big smile on my face. "Hey Sam! Did you order already?"

He led me to a table and says, "Yes. I'm starved." He sits across from me in his blue suit and Snoopy tie. "How's your day going?"

"Great! I have booked The Plain White Tees for a girl's 16th birthday and I have ordered everything for the party. This job is going to be great!"

"I'm glad. You need a good job. You need to pay for my meal every once in a while," he jokes.

I laugh. "I could buy you some different ties."

"What's wrong with my ties? I like Peanuts. It adds life to the newsroom. I brought you an umbrella. It's supposed to rain later."

"Thanks." That's one of the great things about having your best friend as the weatherman. I never have to watch the weather or the news for that matter. I take the umbrella splattered with Peanut characters and put it in my bag. The waitress brings us our pizza and Cokes. Lunch was quiet until Sam brought up the subject of my boss.

"How is your new boss?"

"He's great. I only saw him for the first twenty minutes. He stays in his office a lot. He's really nice and so cute. I hope I get to see him before I go home today."

"L.K., you shouldn't get involved with your boss. Those relationships never end well."

"Who cares?"

"I do. I don't want you to get mixed up with someone who could break your heart and fire you."

"I'm not going to get hurt or fired. I can control myself." We finish our lunch in silence. I don't know what has gotten into him. He has never cared before. After a breakup, he brings cake and I'm good. How weird! It must be that rain that's coming that has got him acting crazy.

"Well, I've gotta run. You want me to come over tonight?"

"Nah, I will probably try to find a roommate tonight. I'll call you though," I say. He kisses the top of my head and walks out of Pete's. I went straight back to the office. I need to find a caterer for this party.

I walk into the office and find Marge sitting behind her desk filing her nails. "Hey Marge! Did you have a good lunch?"

"You bet! A Hot Dog and a Pepsi! How 'bout you?"

"Good. Pete's Pizza and you can't beat that. So, um, can I ask you a question about Mr. Sparks?" I ask.

"Sure."

"Married or single?"

"Involved. He's not married, but I think this one wants to be. She comes by the office a lot. If you hear giggling and the air gets thin, you'll know she's here. Her name is Mindy. She's a tall, brunette, leggy, gold digger," she says.

"Great! Like the world needs another one of those." Crap! "Well, what is his first name?"

"Ben. He's a great boss. You'll like it here. Well, girl, I've gotta finish these nails. Call me if you need me," she says as she continues to file.

I walk back into my office and begin to roll through names of caterers. Paula Deen (too much butter), Bobby Flay (maybe), Emeril (Perfect!). He's quick, he's peppy, and I love the accent! I dial the number and wait for someone to answer. The receptionist transfers my call and I talk with one of Emeril's people. He is a little pricey, but he would definitely be the best. I finally get to talk to someone about getting Emeril. "Yes, I'm calling from Party Central Co and I would like to see if Emeril is available to cater a party," I say with my fingers crossed.

"What day?" the lady asks.

"July 8th"

"Hmm…day or night?"

"Night"

"Hmmm…we would need the theme and times before settling on a price."

"Definitely." I give her all of the details of the party and settle on a price. A big price, but he's going to show up. That's always good. I hung up the phone and did a little dance in my office. BAM! Emeril. This party is going to be a hit!

I notice that is was close to five so I straighten my desk and go to the lounge. I find my mailbox and grab the envelope with my name beautifully printed on it. Ben Sparks' penmanship. I kiss the envelope and open it on my way down the stairs. I look at the amount and fell down the stairs on my butt. $5,000.00!!! I have

$5,000.00! I didn't even notice the pain until I stood up. That is going to leave a mark. I brush myself off and limp to the bank.

I deposit my check and start home. I have had the best day ever! I never want to leave this job. I can't wait until my parents get back so I can rub it in their face. No way am I going to be stuck working at Wal-Mart wearing those blue vests. They were so wrong.

I open the door to my apartment and look in the paper for people wanting a roommate. Fun girl, full time student, cat (NO animals!), Male, 40 (no old dudes!), Female, artist (okay, they don't make money), gay male, stripper (Eww...no!) Female, student, works (Sure, why not). I call the number listed and a man answers the phone.

"Hello," he says.

"Hello. May I speak with Lynsey?" I ask.

"Uh, yes. Hold on." A moment of silence.

"Hello," Lynsey says.

"Hey. I'm calling about your ad. I see you need a roommate. My name is L.K. and I'm looking for someone to move in," I say.

"Hey. I'm Lynsey. Yes, I definitely need a roommate. How much will I need to pay every month?" she asks.

"With rent, utilities, and entertainment it will be around $2000 a month. I live near Central Park so the rent is pricey. Is that something you can handle?" I ask.

"Oh, sure! My parents will be paying for most of it. They want me to get out on my own and meet people. So, when do you want me to move in?"

"Wow, that's quick. I guess anytime you want. I work from 9 to 5, so anytime after 5:00 p.m. or you can come by on Saturday." I told her my address and she said that she would come by on Saturday with her stuff. I hung up and decided to clean Kendra's old room. Lynsey seems nice and I could use some help around here. I just hope that I didn't choose too quickly. She might turn out to be a sports fan or a killer. Yikes!

I turn on the stereo and crank Beyonce's new album and I clean the whole apartment from top to bottom. Lynsey can figure out later that I'm a slob. I hate to clean. I find my chaos more peaceful. When everything is clean, I feel bored.

After cleaning, I felt motivated to exercise. It's probably because of the sweat and the endorphins. I popped in Tae Bo and boxed and kicked until I felt like Muhammad Ali and then I quit and made macaroni and cheese. Something about sweating makes me crave mac and cheese.

I showered and slip into my pink nightie. I plop on the couch to watch Gilmore Girls. I dial Sam's number and wait for him to answer. Hmm….voicemail? "Hey, Sam, call me." I wonder what he is doing. Probably working overtime. The night weatherman stinks!

I think I'll go to bed early. I can read a little and get rested for tomorrow. I read some Beth Moore and thank God for a great day. Then, I am out.

Chapter 4

I awoke to the sound of my phone buzzing. "Hello," I say sleepily.

"Wake up! I need you!"

"Sam?"

"I need you now. Get up! I need you to come into my apartment as soon as possible and bring some tongs or something!" He hung up. Crap! It's only 5:00 a.m. I could have slept until 7:00 a.m.

I get up and quickly take a cab to Sam's. I run up the stairs and unlock his door. His apartment has one recliner and a bed. No other furniture. It screams bachelor except for his kitchen. That is fully stocked. He loves to cook and stuff. "Sam! Where are you?"

"In the bathroom! Come in here quick!"

"I'd rather not!" Ewww. I'm not going in there.

"Just get in here!"

"Fine!" I walk in and I can't believe this. I can't control my giggles. Sam has got his arm stuck in the toilet.

"Stop laughing. I dropped my watch into the toilet and when I went to get it, my arm got stuck."

"You look ridiculous. How did you call me?"

"Pure luck. Just help me. Did you bring tongs or some kind of pulling device?"

"I thought you said thongs and no I didn't bring any."

"Why would I say thongs?"

"I don't know, but I didn't bring any because I didn't want to know what you were going to with them. Plus, I don't own any…I don't think."

"Could you just help me and not try to be funny girl right now?"

I pull and tug and finally get his arm out. It is covered in blue and some unmentionable substances. I gag.

"At least I got my watch."

"Is it any good now? You should have let it go."

"This watch was $900.00. It is my favorite watch and I wear it everyday. I had to rescue it."

"But it's covered in toilet rot now? Oh well, so why didn't you call me back last night?"

"Well, I had to work over and then I met up with the guys to play pool."

"I went to bed early, but you could have called me. I got $5,000.00 in advance pay! I also found out that Mr. Sparks has a girlfriend, Mindy. That sucks. I even cleaned the whole apartment. Well, if you don't need me, I'm going home to get ready for work. Oh, yeah, I got a roommate. Her name is Lynsey. She is a student and is moving in on Saturday."

"Cool. You got a lot accomplished. Thanks for helping me and try not to mention this to anyone."

"Yeah, right! Come over tonight. Bye." I walk downstairs and take a cab home.

I am home by 6:00 a.m. and I decide to go ahead and get ready for work. I take a long bath in my marble tub and scrunch my hair with gel. I put on my khaki capris and a green tank top. I slip on some flip flops and grab a Poptart and a cup of coffee. Time for a day of party planning.

I walk to the elevator and press the down button. The brass doors opened and the tall man is there again. On my bench. This is getting serious. I may have to ask him to move. I walk into the elevator with a feeling of fear. What do I say? "Hey man, that's my bench." I can't say that. So, here goes nothing.

"Um, hello." Real clever, L.K.

"Hello," the man said in a deep, strong voice.

"I'm L.K. Do you live in this building?" Of course he lives here, you idiot!

"Well, sort of. I'm James. I have a studio for when I need to work late."

"Welcome to the building, James. I hope you like it. Can I ask you a question?"

"I guess," he says.

"Can I sit there?" Smooth, L.K.

James stands and allows me to sit on the beautiful bench. "Thank you," I say. "I just need to sit here. I can't explain it." How could you explain it? My only romantic relationship is with an elevator bench. Sad. So sad. Finally, the door opens and I wave to James. I hope he doesn't think I'm weird.

As I enter the office, I notice Mr. Sparks talking to someone. The air feels different. It must be Mindy. They both turn as I enter the room. I wave and head to my office. My face comes into contact with the door and I stumble backward. I hold my head and glance to see if anyone noticed. Three sets of eyes are on me and finally Mr. Sparks asks me if I'm okay. "Yes, I'm fine. Don't worry about me." I walk into my office and close the door and cry. My butt hurts from falling yesterday and know I'm going to have a knot on my head. Crap!

As the embarrassment begins to fade, I begin my calls to confirm location for the party. Micayla's parents have booked the Plaza and I need to make sure everything is okay there. I can't believe this girl is having her birthday party at the Plaza. I think I had my birthday at a Chuck E. Cheese once, which traumatized me for life because Chuck E. Cheese had an asthma attack and had to be rushed out on a stretcher. I still can't go in that place. Anyway, my parents waited until I moved out to get new jobs and become rich in the insurance business. Thanks, Mom and Dad.

I need her guest list so I can make sure everyone gets an invitation. I dial her number. Mr. Jenson answers. "Hi Mr. Jenson! This is L.K., Micayla's party planner. Is Micayla there?"

"Hold on," he says.

I can hear him yell for Micayla and she picks up. "Hello."

"Hey, Micayla. This is L.K., your party planner. Everything is going great! All I need is your guest list and anything else you can think of."

"Well, I'll email my list over, but I would like to make sure that you come to the party and make sure everything goes right. I want security guards, don't forget my cake, I want gift bags for the guests, I want you to pick up my dresses, I'll text you where to pick them up and what time I need them, and I also want you to get me a hair appointment for 2:00 p.m. that day. I know that Daddy has bought me a car, so make sure it has an Egyptian themed bow on top. You got that?"

I had been writing furiously since she started speaking. "Yes, I got it. Anything else?"

"No, just make sure that everything is perfect or my Daddy will sue. TTYL!"

She hung up and I took a deep breath. I have a lot of work to do. What a brat! I can't believe that she just talked down to me that way. Oh well, she's paying. I first arrange for there to be security at her party. That was the easy part. Her email came through. 300 guests! Crap! I told Emeril's people that there would only be 150. That is what her parents told me. Crap! I have to call Emeril!

I dial the number and tell them the change. They were not happy. They are going to charge a lot extra for the last minute change. I make an appointment for her hair and then I begin to decide what to put in the gift bags. I finally decide to fill the bag with truffles, a miniature gold plated King Tut keychain with Micayla's name and birth date on it, an iTunes gift card, a disposable camera, and The Mummy DVD. I considered Mean Girls, but then I decided that might offend someone like the birthday girl. Since I called to order enough for 300 guests, I got a discount. They promised that everything would be here by Friday. I cross my fingers.

For lunch, I decided to eat with Marge. We got a Hot Dog and a Pepsi. I bought an issue of VOGUE and we walk back to the office. "Hey Marge, are you married?"

"Heck, no! I can't stand men. They are too needy. I love living free and single. I can have a boyfriend or I can live without one. How 'bout you?"

"Well, I don't have a boyfriend yet, but I'm looking. Any suggestions?"

"I have a nephew, but he lives in Jersey. What are you looking for?"

"Mr. Sparks. OH! Did I say that out loud?" I ask as my face turns red.

"Yep. I'm afraid so."

"I'm so embarrassed. He's just really hot."

"Well, I can give you some advice. Don't even think about it. If you get involved and things don't work out, you won't be working here. He will fire you on the spot for no reason. That's why you got the job so fast. He fired a girl for coming in late and he needed someone fast. If you ask me, I think that they were involved and he broke up with her. The next day she was gone and he was putting an ad in the paper."

"Hmm…interesting. I thought his last planner left for a mental health thing. Well, I'm going back to work. I have to make sure all of the invitations got here this afternoon. Bye." I walk back to my office and plop into my chair. I don't want to stuff invitations in pyramids all afternoon. I think I will decorate my office. Pottery Barn. Hmmm…I think I'll get online and spend the rest of the day ordering stuff for my office and my apartment. By 5:00 p.m., I had nothing done and I needed the invitations to go out tomorrow. I guess I'll have to take them home. I call a cab and walk out of my office.

On my way out, I bump into Mr. Sparks. "Ben, I mean, Mr. Sparks. I'm sorry."

"Hey, don't apologize. At least I didn't get hit in the nose this time," he laughs.

Man! He is sexy! His laugh is even sexy. "Well, I'm going home. I've got a lot of stuff to do. See ya tomorrow."

He stops me by grabbing my elbow, "Hey, do you have dinner plans tomorrow night?"

Oh man, oh man! "No, why?"

"Well, I was wondering if I could take you to dinner and welcome you to my company the right way," he says.

"Of course I can go. What should I wear?"

"Something nice. I'll have a Limo pick you up at 7:00 p.m. tomorrow night."

"Okay. Thanks"

"No problem. I'll see you tomorrow." With that he touched my shoulder with his hand and walks out the door.

Oh man, Oh man! I'm going to dinner in a Limo with a guy who makes Brad Pitt look like Larry the Cable Guy! With that splendid thought, I put all of the boxes into the cab and start home.

As I walk upstairs, I see Mrs. Tragger. She stops me with her cane and it causes me to trip and drop all of the boxes. "Sorry dear, I just wanted you to come over for a while."

"It's okay. Let me put these boxes in my apartment and I'll be right over." I walk into my apartment and drop the boxes on the floor. I change into my pajamas and walk over to Mrs. Tragger's apartment.

She opens the door before I have time to knock. "Hurry. Friends is about to start. I love that Chandler. He cracks me up! Joke, joke, joke!" I plop down on her old couch and cover up with a quilt that she made. She hands me a plate of meatloaf, potatoes, and green beans. We eat dinner while watching Friends. "May, how did you know that Mr. Tragger was the one for you?"

She says, "He was always there for me no matter what. He would always hold me when I cried. Plus, he bought me things."

"Mmm…"

"Why, Dear?"

"Just wondering. Do you want anything else to drink?"

"No. I need to work on my quilt."

"Well, then I'll let you work. I have lots of work to do too. I'll pick you up on Saturday night. Thanks for dinner."

I entered my apartment and I call Sam so he would come over. It didn't take him long to get here. As soon as he walks through the door, I give him my puppy face. Big eyes, batting lashes, etc.

"What do you want?" he asks.

"Oh, I was just wondering if you could do something for me." I get really close to his face and pout.

"I am not buying tampons again. The last time I did that, I ran into Jake from the station and now I'm called Tampax Man."

"I don't need tampons. I need some help stuffing invitations for this party."

"Oh, well then, okay."

Sam and I stuffed 300 invitations into the little glass pyramids and boxed them in bright blue cardboard pyramids. We added the addresses and the pyramid stamps. Around 1:00 a.m., we finish.

"I don't have to work tomorrow. Do you want me to stay over? Make sure you get up in the morning?" Sam asks.

"Sure. Hey, I have a dinner date with Mr. Sparks tomorrow night."

"You have been working there for two days and he asked you out?"

"Well, not quite. He asked if we could have dinner so he could welcome me to his company."

"So it's a business dinner, not a date. Anyway, didn't you say that he had a girlfriend?"

"Yeah, but I get to go in a Limo. How cool is that?"

"Cool, I guess," he says in a depressed tone.

What's his deal? I never tease him about his dates. Well, maybe I do, but I do it because it's just fun. "Hey, I'm going to bed. Make sure I'm up by 7:00 a.m. Night."

Sam goes to the couch and makes his usual bed and I walk to my bedroom and shut the door.

Chapter 5

I was dreaming about pyramids and cake and I feel my body shaking. I open my eyes to see Sam in my face.

"Get up! Get up!"

"What? You have woken me up like this for two days."

"No, get up! It's 8:15!"

"What?! You were supposed to get me up at 7:00. I have to be at work at 9:00. He fires people for being late. Crap!"

"I overslept. I'm sorry. Get dressed! I'll run you to work in my car."

"Ugh!" I shower quickly and move to my closet! I have nothing to wear! Everything is dirty! Crap! I finally find a pair of blue jean cut-offs and a T-shirt that says "A country girl can survive." With that, I put on cowboy boots. I look in the mirror. Crap! I look like a hillbilly.

Sam drives me to work and tries not to laugh. "Don't say a word."

"I can't help it. You look like Ellie May Clampett! Hey, are we going swimming in the cement pond?"

"Shut up! Just for that, you get to do my laundry while I'm at work and send the invitations."

"Fine, but please let me take a picture before you go." He snaps a shot of me with his phone and I stick my tongue out at him as I shut his car door. I glance at my watch, 9:05. Crap! I'm going get fired on my third day.

I take the stairs two at a time and rush into the office. Marge gives me a "Yee-Haw" and I run into my office. I hope he didn't notice that I was late. I look at all of the boxes in my office. The gift bags. I have to get started on those. As soon as I get up from my chair to start making gift bags, Mr. Sparks walks into my office. "Nice outfit, Ms. London."

"I'm sorry. I haven't had time to do my laundry," I say.

"I think its fine. I couldn't help but notice that you were late today."

"Um, I can explain…"

"No big deal. I just wanted to make sure that everything was okay."

"Oh, yeah, I just had some alarm problems. I won't be late again."

"That's fine. I see everything is going great. When is the party?"

"Next Saturday. I just have a few more details to work out and everything should be fine."

"Make sure you go to the party and put my business card in every gift bag. After lunch, go to Sak's and charge a new outfit to my account. You will need something to wear to the party. When you arrive, they should be holding a couple of things for you to try on to wear to dinner tonight. You can go home after that if you are caught up. Have a good day." With that he walks out of my office. I never

50

get to say goodbye. Oh, well. I get to go shopping on someone else's account. "Loves it," as Paris Hilton would say.

I spent all morning making gift bags and slipping in business cards. I ordered a very Egyptian, very expensive bow to put on top of her new car. I also hired a photographer for the night. All I have to do is pick up her dresses on Saturday and make sure everything gets to the party. My weekend is going to be great!

I grab lunch at a local burger joint and then head over to Fifth Ave. Saks is always so clean. I walk in the door and I'm greeted by a very clean, tall woman. "How may I help you?"

"Um, I am here to try on some dresses for Mr. Sparks," I say.

"Oh, you must be Ms. London. Follow me please. I'm Sandy by the way," she says.

I follow her to a huge dressing room where she and hands me ten dresses to try on. I look at myself in the mirror. Crap! I look like Daisy Duke. I try on every dress and I love every one. Mr. Sparks has great taste! "I don't know which one to choose. I love them all."

"I'll go ring them up," Sandy says as she hands all of the dresses to another employee.

"Oh, wait! I only need two," I say.

"Mr. Sparks said that you were to get anything that you liked. Follow Claire and she will help you pick out shoes and accessories," she says as she walks away.

This is totally awesome! Ben Sparks, you are my new best friend and hopefully, my new boyfriend someday!

I leave Saks with a million bags and I take a cab home. I run everything upstairs and I check my messages. Two from Sam, "L.K., I need to come over before you leave tonight." "L.K., do not leave before I get there." Geez, like I would forget the first message. One from Mrs. Tragger, "Don't forget me tomorrow." One message from my parents, "We have decided to stay in Barbados for another week. Call the hotel if you need us. We love you." Another week. I wonder what is so great that they want to stay another week.

I take a shower to get the nasty, New York cab smell off me and curl my hair. I twist it up to make it look fancy. I wonder where we are going. I put on the black Michael Kors dress and heels. I look in the mirror. Not bad Ms. London.

I hear my door unlock and Sam comes running into the bedroom. "Wow! You look great!" he exclaims.

"Thanks. So, why did you need me to be here?"

"I have a date."

"Okay. This couldn't wait until later?"

"No, I have a date with a girl named Mindy. I met her at the station."

"So, have fun! Wait a minute, did you say Mindy? Like the Mindy? Ben Sparks' Mindy?"

"Yes and she said that her relationship ended suddenly and would like to go out to cheer up."

"Wow. This might be a date after all. Have fun, Sammy!"

"L.K., I really don't think you should get involved with your boss."

"Sam, I don't want to hear this right now. I have a dinner date. I'll call you when I get home. Lock the door when you leave." I left before he could say anything else. I took the elevator. The doors opened and Crap! The tall man, James, is in the elevator again. Is he stalking me? I never get to enjoy the elevator alone anymore. "Hello, James."

"Hey, you want to sit here, right?"

"Please." I take a seat on my bench and enjoy the rest of the trip. The doors open and a say goodnight to James, the bench stealer, and walk out the door. A long, black Limo was waiting for me. Fancy.

A man in a black suit opens the door for me. I slide in and find a letter in the seat with my name on the front. I open the letter and begin to read:

Dear Ms. London,

I hope you will accept the gift inside the box in front of you. Think of it as a welcome gift. See you at dinner.

Ben Sparks

Awesome! Present for me! I open the box and find a diamond necklace. It is so beautiful! There is no way that this thing is real. I put it on and put the letter in my purse. The driver pulls into Per Se on the Upper West Side. Ritzy! He opens the door and helps me out. He says, "Have a good night, Ms. London. Mr. Sparks said that he will take you home."

"Thank you Mr. Limo Driver," I say.

"Bill," he says.

"Okay, thanks Bill." I walk into the restaurant and am amazed by how glitzy everything is. Everything glitters and shines. Even the employees are shiny. I tell the hostess that I am here to meet Mr. Sparks. She leads me to his table. I am way too attracted to him and he looks gorgeous in his Armani suit. He stands as I come to the table. "Hello, Ms. London."

"Hey." We both sit and decide on what to order.

"You look dazzling tonight," he says.

"Thank you! Thank you for everything. I love the necklace and the clothes," I say.

"It was nothing. I need my employees to look their best," he says. "Not like a cowgirl."

"Sorry about that."

"Perfectly fine, Ms. London."

"By the way, you can call me L.K., Mr. Sparks."

"Alright, L.K., you can call me Ben."

We both order lobster and a salad. We talk about the Jenson party while we eat our salad and he seems pleased with my work. I ask about Marge and he just loves her. She has been with him since the beginning of his company. He wouldn't want anyone else. I tell him about my Pottery Barn office and he talks to me about stocks. I have no idea what he said, but the salad was good.

The waiter brings us the lobster. I tell Ben about Sam, my new roommate, and my parents. I notice him looking at me. "I am babbling. I tend to babble when I'm nervous. Tell me about you."

"Well, I was born in Hartford, Connecticut and I went to Yale. (Naturally, all beautiful men come from Yale) I graduated with a business degree and I moved to New York to start some sort of business. I didn't really want to do parties, but it ended up being a gold mine. I'm 27 and I live on the Upper East Side." He continued to tell me about his life and I couldn't help but smile the whole time. He is so fine! I hope this goes well. I haven't spilled anything yet, so I think I'm good.

We finish dinner and I get ready to pay. He waves his hand at me. "This is my treat. Anyone who looks as gorgeous as you do shouldn't have to pay for dinner," he says. I giggle. Oh, my gosh! I just giggled like a little girl. What a moron!

We wait for his car from the valet and he puts his hand against my back. The valet opens the door to a silver Porsche and Ben leads me into his car. As we drive, he turns on the stereo, which is blaring Guns 'n' Roses. He turns it down and looks at me.

"I love Guns 'n' Roses," I say.

"Me too," he says.

He pulls over next to my apartment and gets out of the car. He opens my door and walks me to my door.

"Well, thanks for dinner. It was great! I had a great time. You are a great boss," I say as I open the door. (How many times can you say great before it sounds stupid? I think I passed that point.) He grabs my hand and kisses it. Oh my gosh! I am going to melt right into my Jimmy Choos.

"Thank you, Ms. London. Here, let me get the door for you," he says as he opens the door. I walk in and trip on the rug. My body went to the floor with a slam! I look up and see Ben standing over me. Crap! This is so embarrassing. My chance to be sexy and graceful and I fall on my face!

He helps me up and asks if I need help upstairs. "No thanks. I'll just take the elevator. It's safer."

"Well, I'll see you Monday morning," he says as he walks away.

I have to call Sam. This is great! I get in the elevator and lie on the bench. What a great night! I walk up to my door and I can hear the television. I don't remember leaving it on. Hmm...I unlock the door and I see Sam sitting on the couch. "What are you doing here? I thought you had a date with Mindy."

"I did. She was awful. All she did was talk about Ben. She said that everything was going great and then he just ended it. Apparently, he has met someone else. According to her, he said that he met someone else and had a date tonight."

"Really? Well, things definitely went well. He kissed me!"

"L.K., are you serious?"

"Well, he kissed my hand and he said that I was gorgeous."

"You know this is a bad idea. You need to go to bed and sleep on this. I don't have a good feeling about it."

"Sam, please let me do this. I really like him. He's nice. You see this diamond necklace? Present for me. All of the clothes from Saks? Presents for me. Love is definitely in the forecast, weatherman."

"Please be careful. Goodnight."

"Whatever, Sam." I went to my bedroom and slip out of my dress. I change into a green nightie. I wonder what God thinks about Ben. I guess I'll find out soon.

In the middle of the night, I woke up and felt thirsty. I pattered to the kitchen and noticed that Sam decided to stay the night. I got some juice and turned on the television. I sit on Sam's stomach. He wakes up and I move to sit next to him. He puts his big arm around me and squeezes me tight.

"Sorry," he says.

"It's okay. I just really like this guy and I want your support."

"You have it. Why are you up?"

"I felt thirsty and I can't sleep. I've got Lynsey moving in tomorrow and Bingo tomorrow night. I have church on Sunday and I have one week until the big party. I have so many things going on in my mind." I give him a pout.

"I'll put Signs in," he says as he slips the DVD in. We watched the movie in silence. I must have fallen asleep about the same time that the aliens were invading. I felt Sam pick me up and put me in my bed. What a great friend!

Chapter 6

Lynsey showed up at 6:00 a.m. with her blonde hair, tan body, and bubbly attitude. What time did she get up? I only slept for like three hours. I introduced her to Sam and we met her parents. From 6:00 to 12:00, we helped her unload everything. She has a lot of stuff for one tiny person.

We decided to take a break and get lunch. Her parents took her out for lunch and Sam and I decide to stay here. "So, what do you think of Lynsey?"

"I think she's hot!"

"You cannot date my roommate. That would be too weird."

"So you can date your boss, but I can't date your roommate?"

"That's right! She's nice though, right?"

"Well, she has very nice blonde hair, nice blue eyes, and a nice butt!"

"Sam! No! You cannot date her!" I punch him in the arm. He picks me up and throws me on the couch.

"Fine, but if she asks me out, I'm not going to say no."

"Fine." We made sandwiches and drank lemonade.

After lunch, I told Sam that he needed to go home so that I could bond with my roommate.

"I'll see you at church tomorrow. Bye."

"I'm leaving, but I'm not happy," he says as he leaves.

Lynsey and I unpacked everything and then ordered Chinese. "I love Chinese. Egg rolls, Sesame Chicken, Pon Pon Chicken, Mongolian Beef, everything," I say.

"Me too. It is great college food. It always tastes better the next day," Lynsey says as she stuffs rice into her mouth.

"Exactly. I have to take Mrs. Tragger to Bingo tonight. Do you want to come? It can be pretty dramatic."

"Sure. I love Bingo! What should I wear?" she asks.

"Anything. The place is full of old people. I wouldn't wear anything flashy. You don't want to upset the old men."

She laughs and we get ready. I hand her a key to the apartment and we go to Mrs. Tragger's apartment. I knock softly at her door.

She slams the door open. "Hurry! Move it, London! We have to hurry!" She is wearing pink spandex shorts and an oversized t-shirt with Betty Boop on it. Her scrawny legs move quickly down the stairs even with a cane.

"Hildie May! Slow down!" I scream after her.

"Don't call me that! We have to hurry! Bingo has been moved to SoHo tonight!" she yells.

"SoHo! That will take forever! We'll have to take the subway!" I scream as we move quickly down the street to the subway. Lynsey and I scramble after Mrs. Tragger. We take the subway to Soho and run all the way to the Senior citizen center. We sign in and get our boards. Mrs. Tragger finds seats while Lynsey and I get nachos, popcorn, and root beer. I feel like I just ran a marathon.

"Over here!" Mrs. Tragger waves us over. "Hurry up! Bingo don't wait for nobody!"

"Mrs. Tragger loves Bingo. We do this once a month and she feeds me in return. I thought I would hate it, but we end up having a great time," I tell Lynsey.

"She's crazy and she can move fast for an old lady!" Lynsey exclaims with a giggle.

We head to our seats and I introduce Lynsey to Mrs. Tragger. "Nice to meet you, kid," she says as she hands us pennies out of an old Chinese take out box. She refuses to use the ink dobbers. She claims they make it too fancy.

"What are these for?" Lynsey asks.

"Markers!" Mrs. Tragger shouts.

We all get silent as the caller begins. Mrs. Tragger gets a Bingo every time, like usual. In the middle of the game, when Lynsey taps my shoulder. "Yeah?"

"What is Sam like?" she asks.

"He's cool. Why?"

"I think he's cute. Is he seeing anyone?"

"No."

"Cool."

"Okay." I immediately get back to the game and try to forget the conversation. I mean, I don't care who Sam dates, but I don't want him dating my roommate. That would be awkward and if they broke up, I would have to kick her out. I like Lynsey. I don't want to kick her out.

During the break, I go outside to call Sam.

"Hey! How's Bingo?" he asks.

"Fine, but I'm going to warn you. Lynsey likes you and I think she is going to ask you out. You have to say no. Tell her something. Anything, but don't say yes."

"You are really uptight! L.K., I already told you that if she asks me out, I'm going to say yes. You can have your boss and I'm going on a date with Lynsey."

"Fine, but when things go bad, which they will, I'm not kicking her out."

"Fine. Bye Loser!" He hung up! How rude! I squeeze my way through all of the old people and I sit back down with a thud.

"Is everything okay?" Lynsey asks.

"Yeah." (NOT!)

The game started again. This time you have to cover your board. He is calling all of my numbers! "BINGO!" I shout. I jump out of my seat and I accidentally trip over a chair and land right in the middle of an old man's lap taking him and his toupee down with me. I stand up, toupee in hand, and look around the room. Everyone is laughing and the old man is mad. He grabs his toupee and shoves it back on his head. "You are too clumsy! Get out of my way!" he yells as he shoves me to the ground. He then proceeds to stamp my forehead with a Bingo marker and step on me.

Lynsey and Mrs. Tragger help me up and we decide to leave. I guess that was enough drama for the night.

"You should have pushed that old fart back!" Mrs. Tragger exclaims as we walk back to the subway.

"I can't hit an old man. That would be a crime or something," I say.

"Well, he would have learned his lesson. You can't just start stuff during Bingo. People get upset and we loose Bingo time. Ruth said that he starts trouble everywhere he goes. You should've whacked him with your purse and then tell the police that it was self-defense," she says.

"Whatever. Let's go home," I say as I shake my head. We take the subway and walk back to our building. I hug Mrs. Tragger good night and Lynsey and I go to our apartment.

"So, what did you think of Bingo?" I ask.

"I think it was fun. I also think we should clean your face though."

"Good idea."

Lynsey cleans my forehead and removes the big blue dot. We end up staying up all night talking. We finally fall asleep on the couch watching The Notebook, the most romantic movie of our time I say. It's not like we still have people like Audrey Hepburn making movies anymore. I say Rachel McAdams is the next best thing.

When I woke up, I was practically smothering Lynsey. I quickly jumped up and realized what time it was. 9:00 a.m.! Crap! I'm going to be late for church. I quickly shower and get dressed in one of my new Saks dresses and fly downstairs. I run a few blocks and I see Sam waiting for me on the steps.

"Hey! Why are you late?" he asks.

"I fell asleep on the couch and didn't wake up in time."

"Well, we better get in there. Pastor Tim will pick on us if we walk in late."

We walk into church and find a nice seat in the back. Pastor Tim waves at us and we wave back. We will definitely be picked on. That is the rule with Pastor Tim. He's fun like that.

"Well, I see London and Bridges finally decided to join us this morning. Maybe they would like to help us out in the choir? Can I get an Amen?" Pastor Tim asks the congregation.

We saunter up to the choir loft knowing we can't get away from it and sing our hearts out. The message was good today. He told us about Job and his hardships. I feel very connected to Job right now. We both have had a hard time although I have way better friends than he did.

After church, we took a cab to Greenwich Village and ate at Gray's Papaya. They have the best hot dogs, bar none. Sam and I enjoy our lunch until he brings up the subject of Lynsey.

"So, when is she going to ask me out?" he asks with a sly smile.

"Sam, I don't know. Give it a rest."

"Why? Are you jealous?"

"I think not! I just think it would be weird."

"I don't think it would be. What if she's the one?"

"That's impossible."

"Why L.K.? Why is it so impossible? You can date your "dream" guy and that's possible, but it's not possible for me to be happy?"

"I didn't say that."

"You might as well have."

"I'm sorry. Will you just give it some thought before you say yes?"

"Let's go."

"Fine." We rode back to my apartment in silence. We have been fighting a lot lately, but this time I can tell he is really mad. I don't know what to say. I guess he has the right to date whoever he wants to…I guess. We walk upstairs and he plops down on the couch and turns on the television. Lynsey walks out of her bedroom.

"Where have you guys been?" she asks.

"Church," I say.

"Oh, can I go with you next time?" she asks.

"Sure. I had to rush this morning or I would have asked," I say.

"That's cool. Hey, Sam!" she says batting her eyelashes. Geez.

"Hey Lynsey! You want to watch T.V. with me?" he asks giving me a smirk.

"Sure," she says as she sits beside him.

Oh, great! Sam gives another look and I stomp to my bedroom. I refuse to watch them act like Clark Kent and Lois Lane. I don't know why he insists on this relationship. And she is so giddy. I hate that! I crack open my door and lean against it so that I can watch them. They are laughing, but not at the T.V. Crap! She is touching his arm! How dare she touch his arm! This is getting serious. Oh, she is asking him out! I cannot let this happen. He is saying yes! I knew he would betray me!

As I am thinking of ways to stop them, my arm slips and I crash on the floor right in front of Sam and Lynsey. They look at me and I stand up quickly, brush myself off, and look at them. "I was trying to fix my door."

"You're door is not broken," Sam says as he glares at me.

"Well, the lock was a little punchy," I say as I run back into my room. Crap! I fall on my bed and take a nap. I want to forget this event ever happened.

I wake up to the sound of a door shut. I walk into the living room and Sam glares at me. What's with the glare? I run back into my room and lock the door. He bangs on my door.

"Loralei Katherine London, open this door now!"

"No! And don't you full legal name me either!"

"Yes! We need to talk!"

"No!"

"Open the door now!"

"Fine, but don't you yell at me! I had reasons!" I unlock the door and Sam walks in and sits on the bed.

"You pushed some boundaries," he says.

"It's my apartment."

"It's Lynsey's apartment too."

"It was mine first and you are my best friend. I win."

"L.K., we are going on a date Saturday night while you are at your party. You are going to have to deal with it."

"Oh, great! Give me one more thing to worry about!"

"L.K., I have every right to date her. I think she is nice and I need a date. That Mindy doesn't count. I get lonely."

"Why does it have to be with her? Besides, you can't be lonely…you have me, your best friend."

"I don't know. I'm hot, she's hot. We just click. Yes, we are best friends, but I'm lonely in a different way," he says as he brushes the hair from my face.

"Well, I guess I can deal with that if you really like her."

"I do. I really do."

"Where did she go?"

"She went to her parents' house to pick up a few things."

"Oh. I think I want to go veg out the rest of the day. I feel tired. It has been a crazy day and I have so much to do this week."

"You want me to stay over?"

"No. I don't think it's a good idea that you stay over here anymore with Lynsey being here and all."

"Okay. I'll see you tomorrow. See ya later."

"Night." He left my apartment and I felt sad. I don't know why, but I did. I prayed for guidance and put in a DVD to get my mind off everything.

Chapter 7

Monday morning came too quick. I took a shower and flat ironed my hair. I put on a flippy skirt and a white tank top. I decided to wear my white flip flops with glitter on top. It's summer, why not? I walk in the kitchen and see Lynsey reading the paper. I grab a cup of coffee and sit down beside her.

"Good Morning, L.K.," she says.

"Morning." Where does the cheeriness come from? She must be a cheerleader at college. I drink my coffee and then head off to work. I walk to the elevator and find Mr. Tall once again. "Hey, James!" I exclaim. He nods and moves from the bench so that I can sit. I like this friendship. The doors part and I take off.

I walk into the office and find Marge looking at me in a curious way. "What?" I ask.

"Oh, I was just wondering how your dinner went Friday night," she says.

"It was great. He bought me a diamond necklace and kissed my hand. It was wonderful."

"Huh! Watch yourself, girl! If you like this job, you need to steer clear of Mr. Ben Sparks."

"I love this job, but I don't think he'll fire me. He said he liked my work."

"Whatever," she says as I walk back to my office.

I call everyone on my list to confirm everything for the party. Plain White Tees is ready. Emeril's people said he is a go. Invites are out and gift bags are made and sent to the Plaza. She has a hair appointment and security guards. I decide to hire some men to carry her into her party. Girls like that, right? I would. I finally decide on four Abercrombie models with big muscles and I give them the job. Who wouldn't like that?

At 10:00, I step into the lounge to get some coffee. Mr. Sparks is propped up against the counter drinking coffee. "Hey, Mr. Sparks. I mean, Ben."

"Hello, L.K. How is the party going?" he asks with his sexy smirk.

"Great! I'm basically finished. I just have to show up and make sure everything goes as planned."

"Are you ready for the details of your next party?"

"Sure." I didn't realize I would get another account so fast.

"Follow me." He walks toward his office and I follow. Who wouldn't follow him?

I enter his office and he shuts the door behind us. He hands me a folder and I look inside. It has a picture of a girl and a guy holding hands and smiling. Cassie Mills to wed Jon Meeks. A wedding party! Fun! Big cake!

"I guess you see that you have a wedding to plan," he says.

"The whole wedding?"

"I'm afraid so. It's a big account and we need the publicity. Do you think you can handle it?"

"Of course. I'll go home and watch The Wedding Planner. J-Lo can teach me."

"Well, good luck."

"Okay." I turn to leave and he turns me around. He puts his hand on my cheek. Oh, my gosh! He looks deep into my eyes and kisses me. A deep kiss. A kiss that I will never forget. "Wow!" I whisper.

"Yeah, wow," he says in a hushed tone.

"I'll see you later." I turn to leave and stumble on the rug. I catch myself and keep walking until I reach my office. I fall into my office chair and sigh. What a kiss! I can't wait until I get a repeat! He is super hot! Matthew McConaughey hot!

It was hard to concentrate the rest of the day. I kept thinking about that kiss. Does he want to be more than employer/employee or did that kiss mean nothing? I can't call Sam and ask him. He will just tell me that it's not safe. Lynsey doesn't understand. Marge is already against it. I just need to let go and let God. He'll know how to handle this.

I look through the wedding folder and read all of the details. This is going to be a ritzy wedding and they want to have it in three weeks. What happened? I hope they have all of the invitations out and I hope they have reserved a place to have it. They are pushing time with this wedding, but I already see they are going to be paying for it. Big time. Oh well, I'm just the planner.

After lunch, I play on the Internet until 5:00 p.m. looking at wedding ideas on Pinterest. I walk home and unlock my door. I stop dead in my tracks. Sam and Lynsey are kissing. I can't take this. I'm going shopping. I turn back around and go to Bloomingdale's. What a jerk! He knows that I am against this relationship and he is making out in my apartment with my roommate.

I shop until I can't spend any more money and I start to walk home. I decide to get Chinese first. I can see that they are still kissing so I struggle into my bedroom with my shopping bags and Chinese and I slam the door. I hope Sam can feel my anger. Crap! I need a Dr. Pepper. I run into the kitchen, grab two DPs, and fly back into my bedroom. I pop in The Wedding Planner and eat. While J-Lo is giving me the 411 on wedding planning, I fall asleep.

I hear my door open and I feel someone sit beside me. I glance at the time. 3:00 a.m. Ugh! I know its Sam. I ignore him. He touches my shoulder. I ignore him. He tugs a strand of my hair. I flip over and glare at him. "What Sam?"

"I'm sorry."

"For what? You have nothing to apologize for. This is Lynsey's apartment too, remember?"

"I know, but I knew you wouldn't want to see us kissing."

"Oh well! Be with Lynsey! I don't care! Ben kissed me today in his office. I have somebody. Love whomever you want! Good night, Sam!" With that, I turn around and cry. I don't know why. I just feel like crying. Sam picks me up and holds me. He strokes my hair until I fell asleep. I felt him move and I heard the door shut. Good night, Sam, you roommate loving moron!

I got up the next morning and decided to call in. I feel awful. I need more sleep and time to think. Normally, I would spend the 4th of July with friends eating hot dogs and watching firecrackers, but I definitely don't feel like getting out of bed. I don't want to face today and the trouble that goes with it. I don't want to see Ben right now. What if he doesn't want me? I can't deal with that right now. I call the office and Marge answers, "Party Central Co. can I help you?"

"Marge, this is L.K. I am sick. I'm all caught up with the party. Besides, it's Independence Day! Can you tell Mr. Sparks that I won't be in today?" I ask.

"Sure, but he don't like call ins. Especially on the holidays," she says.

"I don't care. I feel like crap and I need sleep," I say.

"Okay. Feel Better. Bye." She hung up.

I go back to sleep and I wake up at 12:00 because someone is knocking loudly at my door. Where is Lynsey? Why is she not answering the door? She's probably out with Sam! Ugh! I don't want to think about that either. I fall out of bed and walk to the door. "Who is it?!" I yell.

"Ben."

Crap! Why is he here? I can't be seen like this! "Hold on!" I yell. I run to the bathroom and fix my hair. I run back to the door and open it. He is holding a bag.

"May I come in?" he asks.

"Uh, sure." He walks in and hands me the bag. I open the bag and pull out a bowl of soup. "Thanks."

"I heard you were sick," he says.

"I was. I feel better now. What are you doing here? Don't you have to work?"

"I wanted to make sure you were okay. Marge can hold down the fort for a while. We don't have many calls on the 4th. Nice apartment."

"Thanks. My roommate is a neat freak. She keeps the whole place clean. Do you want to sit down?" The apartment is decorated with Stars and Stripes. Lynsey likes to decorate for the holidays apparently.

"Sure." We sit on the couch and he puts his arm around me. I sit closer to him and he kisses my head. I look up at him and he kisses me passionately. I pull away. "Can I be serious with you?"

"Of course," he says.

"I like you, but I need to know that you like me and that our relationship is not going to interfere with our work relationship."

"I like you too. This is not going to be a problem. When we are at work, we are employer/employee. Is that okay?"

"Yes."

"Can I kiss you again?"

"Of course." He kissed me. He pulled the stars and stripes blanket over me, and told me to sleep. I feel so comfortable. I hear the door open and I can hear Lynsey and Sam talking. I decide to keep my eyes closed and just listen. I don't want to look at Sam right now.

"I don't know you, but since my best friend is lying on your lap I have to assume you are L.K.'s new boss," Sam said with a sarcastic tone.

"That's me. I'm Ben Sparks. You must be Sam and Lynsey," Ben says.

"What's wrong with L.K.?" Sam asks.

"She didn't feel well so I came over to bring soup," he says.

"She likes cake," Sam says in a possessive tone. Why is he being rude? Ben is being so nice.

"Well, she seemed to enjoy the soup," Ben replies. Actually, I didn't. It had vegetables in it.

"If she is sick, maybe she needs to go to bed," Sam says.

Ben says, "She seems comfortable to me. Maybe you guys should let her sleep."

Even with my eyes closed, I know that Sam is steamed. I love it! "Well, put her in the bed then," Sam scolds.

"I don't want to wake her."

I feel Sam's presence. "Then I'll do it." Sam's arms lift me and place me on my bed. Crap! I don't want his roommate loving hands touching me. I can still hear them talking.

"I think I'll be going now. Tell L.K. I will see her in the morning." With that, he left. Crap! Sam, you idiot! Why can't you let me have any fun?

"Can you believe that guy?" Sam asks Lynsey.

"What? We should be happy for her. He's hot." I knew I liked that girl.

"I just think that he seemed a little off. I don't want L.K. to get hurt. He seems like the heartbreaking type."

"I think we need to trust and support L.K. and her decision. He seemed nice to me. Well, I've got to run to school and get registered. My senior year is going to be tough and busy and I want to try to take some of the load off. See ya later," she says. I could hear her kiss him. Yuck!

I could hear Sam tip toe into my room. He sat on the side of my bed. I wonder if I should ignore him or wake up and face the music. I shift over and look at him. "What?"

"Do you feel better? Can I get you anything?"

"No, what's wrong?"

"Nothing. I met your boss. Nice guy." I know he's lying. I can tell by the wrinkle in his forehead.

"Yeah. He's really nice, Sam. I think you'd like him if you got to know him better."

"You have had one date. Give it some time before you decide anything. Okay?"

"Whatever. What about you and Lynsey?"

"It's great. I can't wait until Saturday. We are going to have a blast. I'm taking her to Peter Lugar's Steak House. Then, I'm going to take her dancing. Do you think she'll like it?"

"I'm sure she will." I like dancing. He has never taken me dancing. Wait a minute! Why would he? We aren't dating or anything weird like that. We are just friends. Like Monica and Rachel or Joey and Chandler.

"Well, I'm going to let you sleep. Feel better. Happy 4th!" He pats my head and leaves. The air feels different. I decide to read a little from Ephesians and forget about the weirdness of today.

Chapter 8

The rest of the week flew by and Saturday hit me like a ton of bricks. I woke up at 4:30 a.m. and got dressed in jeans and a t-shirt. I'll come back home and change before the party. I took a cab to the Plaza and began working.

I made sure that everything was going as planned. The dogs, the panthers, the gift bags, her dresses are hung up in her dressing room and have been steamed, the security guards, the models, etc. Plain White Tees are here and rehearsing. I am so psyched about this! Emeril's crew is working hard and getting everything BAMMED UP!

One of the decorators asks me where I'm going to put the cake. Crap! The cake! I didn't order a cake! What am I going to do? Crap! I call Sam, "I forgot to order the cake!"

"What? What are you going to do?"

"I don't know! That's why I called you! Give me a solution!"

"I don't have any. You're the party planner. Go to a near by bakery and see if they can throw something together before the party."

"Good idea. Bye!" I hang up and run furiously through the street and find a bakery. I rush in and knock a lady over. "Sorry! So Sorry! No time!" I run up to the counter and plead with the baker. "Please. I need an Egyptian themed cake to feed 300 people by 5:00 p.m. No money limit! I am desperate!"

"You should have ordered a cake weeks ago. I am afraid that I can't help you," the woman says.

"Please. I am begging you. I just need a cake in the shape of a pyramid or something. I can't believe that I forgot the cake. Cake is my favorite thing about birthday parties. If everything doesn't go as planned, Mr. Jenson will sue my boss and my boss, who happens to be my maybe boyfriend...will fire me. I love my job and my boss.

I can't let anything go wrong. My best friend is dating my roommate. I just don't know if I can handle it! Please, oh, please make this cake," I say. I am frazzled and I don't know what to do. I can't bake a cake. I can't boil water without burning it!

The woman holds up her hand and stops me before I can go on, "Fine. I'll help you, but this is going to cost you. Big."

"Oh thank you. Thank you. Thank you!" I exclaim. I gave her a huge hug and told her that I would pick it up in a few hours.

I call Sam, "Cake disaster solved."

"Great! What should I wear tonight?"

"Sam! I don't care what you wear. I need soothing right now. I need comfort. I absolutely could care less about what you wear on your date with Lynsey!"

"Lora Kate! Calm down! You are screaming at me. Are you mad about my date with Lynsey?"

"No. Yes. No, I'm not mad. I just need to get some coffee. I want a big cup of coffee. I'll talk to you later." I hung up and went to get coffee.

I walk into a little café and wait in line. I finally get my turn to order. "Me. Coffee. Now." The waitress knew my language and handed me a huge cup of Joe. I turn around and there is Mr. Tall. Does he follow me? This is New York City after all. You are not supposed to bump into people more than once unless you plan it. He could be a stalker. Even though, if anyone stalked me for long, they would realize that I have no money to steal. Oh, wait, that's a mugger, not a stalker. Oh, well.

"That will be $4.50," the waitress says.

"I'll get it," James says as he hands her a $5 bill.

"Thanks," I say. Stalker, definitely.

"You want to sit for a minute?" he asks as he gets a cup for himself.

"Um, sure." No! Stalker Guy! But I don't want to be rude. At least we are in public. We sit in a corner booth under a large picture of a dog, which is strange because dogs and coffee have nothing in common. Hmm...

"So, other than demanding an elevator bench, what do you do?" James asks.

"I am a party planner. This is my first party and I forgot the cake, but everything is fine now. How about you? What do you do?" I ask.

"I sort of run a business," he said.

"Cool. Are you married?" I ask. I don't why.

"Maybe. Are you married?"

"No. I have a boyfriend though, a strong one." Better to be safe that sorry, right?

"Is he the young man with the wild hair?"

"Oh, no. That's my best friend, Sam. He is currently dating my new roommate, which, by the way, I'm totally fine with."

"I can tell. So, Ms. Party Planner, do you think you could plan a party for me sometime?"

"Sure!" I hand him Ben's business card. "I would love to plan a party for you. Call us and we will set it up." We spend the next two hours talking about weddings, parties, and everything that goes with that. I glance at my watch! Crap! I have to pick up the cake and get changed. I also want to see Lynsey and Sam before they leave. "I have to go! I have so many things to do! I'm sorry! I'll see you in the elevator! Bye!" Okay, not a stalker. I run to the bakery and pick up the cake. It is wrapped in a huge box. I hope this works out. I take the cake to the Plaza and take a cab home.

I bolt up the stairs and shower quickly. I put on a pink dress perfect for dancing and looking professional. The back is cut out so I have to wear those sticky bra things. I hate those. I slip on pink stilettos and curl my hair up into a twist. I put on my diamond necklace that Ben got for me and Mom's diamond earrings. I hope I look fancy enough to blend in. As I put on the finishing touches of my makeup, there is a knock at my door. "Come in!"

Lynsey walks in, "You look great!"

"Thanks! You do too!" She is sporting the "college look." You know, the little halter top and the skirt with the big hooker boots. So weird.

"Sam is taking me to dinner and then dancing. He is supposed to show up any minute."

"I hope you have a great time." Not! I don't know why I am so against them being together. I love Lynsey! She is a great roommate. She cleans, she cooks, and she even pays the bills. She said that if I give her money that she would take care of everything. I couldn't ask for a better roommate. I have got to shake this! There was a knock at the door and Sam walked right in.

"Well, there's Sam. Have a great night!" she smiles.

"You too." Whatever!

I stroll out of my room and I look at Sam. He is dressed up and she is dressed like a lady of the night! He must really like this girl. "Sam, you look nice," I say.

"You too. You are shiny," he says.

"I hope that's a compliment. Well, I have to go to my party. Wish me luck!"

I go to the elevator and press the down button. I try to calm my nerves by shaking my arms in the air. The door opens and Ben is there. He takes my hand. "What a surprise! I didn't think you would be here."

"Well, I wanted to see you. You look beautiful. Are you nervous?"

"Yes! Are you coming to the party?"

"Of course. You need a date. I don't want anyone thinking that you are single." He kisses me and puts his arm around me until the elevator opens. He opens the car door for me and we travel to the Plaza.

The place is already buzzing. Everything looks great! I did it! I planned this party! I made this happen! Micayla Jenson is going to be surprised when she finds out The Plain White Tees are performing and Emeril is feeding everyone.

The gift bags are sparkling under the chandelier. The black panthers are in cages decorated with bows. Scary. Everyone is dancing. I notice the cake glittering on the table. Thank goodness! The party is a hit!

Mr. Jenson is walking toward us. "Hi! I'm L.K., the party planner. What do you think?" I have to shout. It is so loud.

"Terrific! Micayla is very pleased. Looks like you missed a lawsuit! She is getting a BMW convertible tonight! By the way, I received the bow! How did you know about the car?" he asks.

"Intuition, I guess!" I yell.

"Is that Emeril cooking in the kitchen?" he asks.

"Yep! The Plain White Tees are going to perform. It's a surprise!" I scream. It keeps getting louder in here.

"Perfect! I knew I made the right choice. Mr. Sparks, you have got a good one here!" he says.

Ben says, "I know. I won't ever let her go." Oh, job security! Sweet! Wait a minute, did that mean commitment? Yikes!

"I'll send my check on Monday! L.K., you just got yourself a bonus. I'll be calling again when Micayla turns 21. Have a good night!" With that, he walked away and found someone else to talk to.

Sweet! I get a bonus! I turn and face Ben. He smiles at me and kisses my forehead. "Good work, Ms. London. I think I should promote you to head party planner."

"You mean there are other party planners?"

"Of course! You didn't think I got rich by having one party every once in a while, did you?"

"I guess not. How many planners do you have?"

"Around 15 right now, but I'm hoping to have more by the end of the year."

"When you hired me, you said that you needed someone quick. Why couldn't you get someone else do the party?"

"I don't like to double book my employees. I like everyone to focus on one event at a time. I don't want anyone working on an out of state party and have to worry about an inner city event."

"We do out of state parties? Do they attend the parties that they plan?"

"Of course! That is my rule. Attend the event for publicity."

"Awesome! Since I'm being promoted, do I get to work on out of state stuff?"

"Maybe, but I'd rather you do inner city stuff. That way you are closer to me."

"Good plan." Before I can say anything else, I hear the drums. It's time for Micayla's big entrance.

The room fills with a fog and the Abercrombie models come out carrying Micayla on a large fluffy bed. She is wearing a gold dress and two pointy-eared dogs are on each side of her. Everyone oohs and awes over Micayla. Great, another brat with great legs. That's all we need in the world.

Ben slips his arms around my waist and whispers, "Good job." Then he kisses my ear. We watch Micayla rule her party. She is having a blast! The food looks amazing. Emeril really kicked it up a notch! I love Food Network lingo. EVOO, shallots, nutmeg, kale, couscous. What is couscous? The Plain White Tees walk on stage and the whole place is filled with screams. "I think it's a hit, don't you?" I ask Ben.

"Definitely! Hey, I have to go check my e-mail. I'm waiting to hear from some people in Orlando. I'll come back to pick you up at 11:00 p.m. Okay?"

"Okay." I give him one of my famous pouts and he kisses me. I walk him to the door and feel the hot, July air kiss my face. He walks away and I turn around to check out the party when all of a sudden, I am knocked down by many screaming teenagers. Crap! Someone just kicked me! "Hello! Person on the ground!" I scream, but no one can hear me. I can only guess that Micayla got her birthday present. I finally pick myself off the ground and look down. Great! My dress is ruined. I have to get out of here. I have done my job. My skirt is ripped and dirty. Crap! I don't have a ride and I have to stay here until 11:00. Wonderful!

I go to the kitchen and try to find some scissors. I rummage through the drawers and cabinets. Bingo! I grab the scissors, which I'm sure are for cutting chicken or something, but I don't care. I'm desperate. I have to fix this dress. I glance around and see no one. Maybe they all left. Good. I slip my dress off and start cutting away.

In mid project, I hear a cough. I'm afraid to look up. What do I do? Should I grab my dress and run or should I just look up? Run? No, then I'll have to go through the party. Look up? Why not? Crap! I look up and see the entire kitchen staff along with Emeril staring at me.

"Sorry. I had a wardrobe malfunction. A Janet Jackson moment." I slip the dress on quickly and apologize once again. I move fast out of the kitchen and then hear a roar of laughter erupt. Great! Emeril and his crew just saw me in my underwear. Crap!

I decide to hide in the bathroom for the rest of the party. I cut the dress too short so my butt shows. I blame Sam for this. I wonder what he's doing now. I'll call him. He'll love it. I dial the number and wait.

"Hello!" he yells.

"Hey! Why is it loud there?" I ask.

"We're dancing! How did the party go?"

"The party went great, but I was knocked down, I flashed Emeril, and I ripped my dress."

"What? I can't hear you! I'll talk later! Bye!" He hung up! How rude! I was trying to tell him about my awful night and he hangs up to dance. Fine!

I sit on one of the bathroom sinks and cross my legs. I check my watch. 10:55. I'm calling Ben. "Ben, where are you?"

"I'm walking in the door. Where are you?"

"I'm in the bathroom. Could you find an unused table cloth and come get me?"

"I'm afraid to ask. I'll be there in a minute. Bye."

He walks into the bathroom and smiles at all the paper towels wrapped around my legs. "What happened?"

"The minute you left, 300 teenagers trampled me to see the shiny car. The fall ripped my dress. I went to the kitchen to find scissors so that I could fix my dress. I thought everyone had left so I took my dress off so that I could cut it. I was wrong. I flashed Emeril and I cut my dress too short. I want to go home." He covered me with the tablecloth with a big grin on his face. He led me to his car and went inside to thank everyone.

When we got to my building, he carried me to my apartment in the tablecloth labeled "Property of the Plaza." I break the silence, "So, fun night?"

"It's never a dull moment around you. Hey, I have something for you."

"For me?" Hurray! A present! For me! He hands me a little blue bag. I know little blue bags. Little blue bags come from Tiffany's. I slowly take out the small box and open it. "Oh, pretty!" It's a small charm in the shape of a cupcake with little diamond sprinkles and it's attached to a gold chain.

"I heard that you like cake, so I wanted you to have cake at all times. Read the back."

I turn the charm over and find an engraving, "A little frosting for my love." Oh my gosh! I am in love! "Ben!" He puts the necklace around my neck. I hug him tight and kiss him. He picks me up and twirls me around. I feel like a princess. This is the perfect moment, like a Cinderella moment in a fairy tale.

As soon as the thought leaves my mind, the door opens. Crap! Lynsey and Sam. They ruined my moment. Ben and I go to my bedroom and close the door.

"Babe, I have to go. Kiss me before I leave," Ben says as he takes me in his arms. I kiss him and tell him good night. He called me, Babe. Is it too soon to start pet names? As soon as he leaves, I change into a yellow nightie and cover myself with a matching robe. I'm not tired. I'm going to go in the living room and watch television.

I walk in to see Lynsey and Sam kissing again on my couch. I have had it. I want to watch television in the living area. This is where we do the whole living thing. I clear my throat and they both look up.

"Sorry, L.K. We were just saying good night. I want to get plenty of sleep. So…." Lynsey says as she kisses Sam good night. She walks to her bedroom and shuts the door.

"Hey, so tell me about your party," Sam says.

"Well, do you want to hear the long version or the short version?"

"Short version and then tell me the long."

"I got trampled by teenagers, I flashed Emeril, and I cut my dress too short so I felt like Lindsay Lohan at the Nickelodeon Kid's

Choice Awards. It was fantabulous, but I did get this from Ben." I show him my necklace and he rolls his eyes.

"I told him that you liked cake, you know."

"So."

"I just think that it was a cheap way to get closer to you."

"Okay. So you and Lynsey can be Superman and Lois and I can't get a present from my boyfriend without hearing your opinion. I don't think so. I'm going to forget what you said." I wiggle my nose like Samantha from Bewitched and erase the moment. "I told you not to date my roommate. Now everything is weird."

"I told you not to date your boss, so this is not all my fault. So, you think I look like Superman?"

"Ugh! That is so not what I meant. Oh well. You're happy and I'm happy!" I spend the next two hours eating ice cream and telling Sam all of the details of the party. Then, he went home and I slept on the couch.

Chapter 9

Church was great on Sunday. Lynsey came with us and Pastor Tim told us about being the light of Jesus around us. As the sun rose on Monday morning, I was determined to be a light. I was going to change my attitude about Sam and Lynsey. I am going to be in a good mood from now on. I am going to plan a wedding for Cassie Mills and Jon Meeks. It is going to be great! I tell God my plan, which I'm sure made Him laugh because His plans are better and make more sense than mine do.

I figured that I would be on the phone all day, so I dressed in khaki shorts and a purple tank top. I did the ponytail and lip gloss thing. I walk into the kitchen and Lynsey is making breakfast. "Good morning, Lynsey!"

"Morning. What's with the cheery mood?"

"I am starting a new life. I am going to be the best person I can be. I'm going to be a happier person."

"Sounds good! You want some breakfast?"

"Sure. I'll take some bacon on toast with coffee. I have to run. I want to start early today." Lynsey wraps everything up for me and I grab it. "Thanks, Mom!" I yell as I run out.

I go to the elevator. James is there again. "Hey, James!" He stands from the bench and I sit and eat. "What's up?"

"I'm going to work. You?"

"Me too. I have a wedding to plan."

"Sounds fun! Is Mr. Sparks working you too hard?"

"Nope! He is great! I am great!" The doors part and I hop out. I wave to James and head to work.

Marge is sitting at her desk reading a trashy novel. I wave to her and skip to my office. I plop down in my comfy Pottery Barn chair and start looking through my wedding file. This is great! I turn my iPod on and listen to Bowie. I'm chillin'. I'm groovin'. I'm singin', "Ground control to Major Tom. Commencing count down, engines on. Take your protein pills and put your helmet on... I look up to see Ben smiling at me. I giggle. "Sorry. I got lost in Bowie world. What's up?"

"Well, I'm glad that you are in a good mood. I have some good news for you. Since you have been promoted to head party planner, I have decided to give you a new account."

"I thought you didn't want to double book your planners?"

"Oh no, you will no longer be planning the Mills/Meeks wedding."

"I thought I was promoted. Why are you taking my wedding away? I watched Jennifer Lopez and everything."

"I have something better."

"Oh, I like the sound of that. Please fill me in."

"I want you to close your eyes and think about the sun, the ocean air, a castle, Mickey Mouse…"

"Oh my gosh! I'm going to Disney World! What's going down in Disney World?" I ask as I hop up and down.

"Well, we are going to Orlando to plan a birthday party for a 7 year old girl named Storm."

"Like the weather event?"

"Yes. You may invite two guests and we are leaving Friday. I want you to work on getting us travel arrangements. Use my name to get the good stuff. Don't waste time. You need to get everything booked by 5:00 p.m. today. You can have the rest of the week to do research on Orlando and find all of the places where we can get stuff for the party. This is a huge account. They are paying double since it is last minute. They have reservations already made for some places. Everything you need is in the binder. Study it and figure out how to give Storm the best party. We will be there for one week and two days. Take Thursday off for packing. I'm counting on you, Babe. By the way, I will be super busy this week, so I probably won't get to see you until Friday."

I give him a pout, "But, I will miss you." He reaches over and kisses me and hands me the party binder. Everything comes in a binder around here and he talks so fast. I'm glad everything does come in a binder because I could never remember everything he says.

"I know, but we will see each other everyday next week. It will be great. I assume you are going to be bringing Sam and Lynsey?"

"Yeah, they would kill me if I didn't."

"Book two rooms, a room for us and a room for the other two. Make sure they join. Try to get something in Disney World so that we are near the party, okay?"

"Okay, but Lynsey and I will share a room and you can share with Sammy. I can't believe we are going to Florida! This is going to be great! I get to work and play. I'll see you Friday." He kisses me and leaves. He always comes in and makes a long speech and then leaves. I feel like I have to take notes every time we speak.

I call Sam. He is going to be so psyched! "Hey, what are you going to be doing on Friday?"

"I don't know. I will probably take Lynsey out," he says.

"Wrong! You are taking a vacation."

"What? I'm not going on vacation. What's going on?"

"Well, I've got a new party to plan and it happens to be in Orlando. And I happen to get to invite two guests."

"Awesome! Is Lynsey going?"

"Okay, you ruined it. I invite you to go and all you can think about is Lynsey."

"Sorry, but I figured that you would invite us both. How long are we staying?"

"One week and two days. Take vacation now and you can call Lynsey and tell her we are going. You're welcome!" I hang up and start making reservations.

I find three different places that sound great! I don't know which one to choose. I pick up the phone and punch in Ben's extension. "Do you want to stay at the Animal Kingdom Lodge, Disney's Yacht Club, or The Grand Floridian?"

"Um, which one do you like?" Ben asks.

"I think the Animal Kingdom Lodge looks cool. You can get a two-bedroom suite that overlooks the animals. It looks very cool, but it seems too expensive. I mean, $1,140 a night seems pretty outrageous, right?"

"If you like it, then it doesn't matter. Book it! I've got L.A. on the phone. I'll talk later. Bye."

I hang up. Wow, he's got the whole city of L.A. on the phone and all I have to do is make reservations for a week and two days. I am so excited. The lady on the phone said that with our purchase, we get into all of the parks. I can't wait. I call JFK and get our plane tickets.

Since Ben is busy, I'm going to eat lunch with Sam today. I'll meet him at the station. I take a cab over to the news station and hop into the weather room. I sneak behind Sam and cover his eyes. "Guess who?"

"E.S.?" he asks.

"No. It's me." I pull my hands away and he turns around and smiles. "Who is E.S.?"

"You. I kind of told the whole station about your Emeril moment and somebody called you the Emeril Streaker. I thought it was funny."

"I'm so glad that you and your coworkers delight in my pain. It gives me a bubbly feeling inside."

"I'm so glad. So, what's up?"

"I thought we could go to lunch?"

"Sure. Let me wrap things up. I'll meet you in the lobby."

I walk past the giggling weathermen and news anchors and go into the lobby. I sit on the green, leather sofa and cross my legs. I wonder why Sam needs to wrap things up. I don't even know what that means. I see him running towards me. "Hurry! If we don't go now, they'll stop me." He grabs my arm and drags me to his car.

"Why are we running again?" I ask.

"Something messed up on the computer and I'm the only one who knows how to fix it. I had to get out of there."

"You seem mad."

"I'm not," he says as we drive out of the car lot.

"Yes, Oscar, you are."

"I'm not mad. I just hate when they do that. Someone else needs to learn how to use the computer. It's the 21st century. You'd think that everyone would know how to use a computer by now."

"Not everyone is a genius, Mr. Gates."

"I guess."

"Where are we going?"

"Pete's."

"What's going on with your hair, Axel Rose? You going for the rocker look?" I ask as I toss his long, sandy hair.

"Lynsey said that she likes guys with long hair."

"Well, I like the wild look that you had before. Cut it! It's heinous!"

"Fine! I'll get an appointment before we leave on Friday." Satisfaction! I always get my way. We get out of the car and walk in. I find a table while Sam orders. I hope he gets a pie with pepperoni, sausage, and cheese. Sam walks over and shoves hair from his face. "So, tell me about Florida. Where are we staying?"

"Animal Kingdom Lodge. It's very expensive and it's so nice. We leave JFK at 1:00 p.m. It was the best that I could get. Did you put in for vacation?"

"Yep! Lynsey is excited too. She cancelled her first summer course."

"We have a 2 bedroom suite. Lynsey and I get to stay in the room with the biggest bathroom. I love the tub."

"Did you choose the room because of the tub?"

"Of course! We get passes to every park! This is going to be so great! I have to spend the rest of the week planning, but I get to take Thursday off so I can pack. I think this is what we all need. We should watch Signs tonight to celebrate."

"Can't. Lynsey and I are going to some poetry reading at Java's. You can come if you want?"

"Sam, I got fired from there. I can't go."

"Sorry. You could go though. You have a new job now. You don't have to worry about them."

"I'm still not going. They might serve me a sneeze-muffin. I'm not chancing it."

After lunch, Sam dropped me off at the office. I walk in and decide to see where Ben hides all of these party planners. I tiptoe through the hallway. Each office has a huge window so that you can look in without having to go into the office. I see many men and women talking on headsets and writing stuff down. One girl looks up at me and I wave. She waves back and I continue to walk and the hallway ends. There is an elevator. Cool! I press the up button and get in. It has a bench! It's different from the one in my building. It is purple and red and has gold feet. I sit down and I wait.

The door opens and I'm in a hallway. I'm lost. I keep walking and I see Marge. "Hey! Did you know that there is an elevator?"

"Well, yeah!"

"Oh, I just found out that there is a whole floor of planners down there."

"What did you think was down there?"

"Aliens."

"Girl, you are crazy! I heard that you are going to Orlando."

"Yep! I'm excited! Ben and I get to spend a whole week together. He is always so busy. I hardly get to see him."

"He stays on the phone all day. He will probably be on the phone in Orlando. I can't believe that he is going with you. He normally never leaves the office unless he needs to."

"He must really like me, huh?" I show her the necklace that he bought for me.

"Nice. Tiffany's?"

"Yeah, how did you know?"

"Just a guess."

"Well, I need to find out all of the details to this party. I'll see you later."

I walk to my office and find a million messages about the new party. Storm's parents, Hilary and Scott Finn, want Cinderella's Castle for the party. I didn't know you could do that. I found out that the theme is Disney Princesses. Big surprise! Her parents want me to plan the party and order the cake. I have to order gift bags, a singer, a castle cake, and I have to arrange for all of the Disney

Princesses to attend. They want a fireworks display and dinner at Cinderella's Royal Table for all 200 guests. I'm going to be busy this week.

At 5:00, I went into the lounge and grab my paycheck. I'm never going to get used to being paid whenever I get a message about it. It's strange. Oh, well. It pays the bills and gives me extra to spend on fun things.

I deposit my check and go home. I leave an envelope with money for the month on Lynsey's desk. She pays the bills and gets the groceries. I love it! I have no responsibility in this apartment except myself and my dirty clothes. It's great.

I grab FIJI water and I decide to call my parents. They were supposed to be back from Barbados today. It rings six times and my mother's maid, Gerta, answers. "Hello. Zis is zee London residence," she says in her thick German accent.

"Gerta, it's Lora Kate. Are my parents back yet?"

"Nein. Mrs. London called yesterday und said zat zey decided to go to Europe. Somezing about cheese. She said zat you should call zem on her new cell phone. Here is zee number. Are you ready?"

"Sure." I jot down the number and then call it. "Mom, its Lora Kate. Where are you?" I ask.

"Rome! It's fabulous! How are you?" she asks.

"Fine! I got a new job. I'm a party planner now. It's glamorous. I'll be in Orlando next week. I thought you should know. Why are you in Rome?"

"Oh, I'm so proud of you, Lora Cake. We decided to spend the rest of our summer in Rome. The States can be so boring during the summer. The Kellermans bought a summer villa here and they invited us to stay with them. Did you call the house?"

"Yeah."

"Was Gerta there?"

"Yeah." Where else would she be?

"Wonderful! She is packing more things to send to us. I told her she could stay there with her husband while we are gone. We get to travel and my house stays clean. They are staying in the guest room. Go over and check things out every once a while, could you?"

"Sure. I'm glad you and Daddy are having a great time. I have a new boyfriend. He's my boss, but things are fine."

"Well, I'm happy. You be careful Lora Cake. Daddy sends his love. I'll bring presents for you. I love you. I have to go. Bye, love!" And she's gone. My parents have gotten strange in their old age.

I order Chinese from across the street. "Hello. May I take order?"

"Yes. I need egg rolls, shredded beef, sesame chicken, soup, and Mongolian beef," I say.

"For one person?"

"Yes. Don't judge me! Just deliver it!" I tell him my address and I wait. I change into an orange nightie and paint my toenails.

I'm feeling kind of adventurous. I find my copy of The Wizard of Oz and slip it into the DVD player. Just as Dorothy confirms that she's not a witch, my Chinese arrives. I pay the man and continue my movie. I eat half of everything and stick the rest in the fridge.

Just as Dorothy clicks the ruby slippers, I hear the lock turn. Crap! I grab my robe. As I put it on, Lynsey and Sam walk in crying. Lynsey kisses him deeply and hugs him. It's like HBO at night in here. I watch the drama and wonder what's going on. She walks back to her bedroom and shuts the door. Sam turns to leave and I stop him. "Hey!"

"Oh, L.K. I didn't know you were here." He walks over and sits beside me.

"What's with the water works, Weepy?"

"The poetry reading was emotional."

"Well, cry me a river, Justin. I'm sure Britney Spears will be happy," I can't help but giggle. That was a good one!

"It's not funny. Lynsey has helped me find my inner artist."

"That's dumb! Move to The Hills for the drama or watch Grease with me."

"Fine, but I'm not singing along."

"Yes you are, Travolta," I say as I pop in Grease.

Chapter 10

I wake up on Tuesday with a smile. I am so ready to go to work! I shower and dress in a silky, black top and a flippy skirt. I curl my hair and add mascara. I decide to wear heels today. Why not?

"So fancy," Lynsey says as I walk to the kitchen.

"Thanks. I'm hoping that dressing nice will motivate me to get busy on this party." I quickly drink a cup of coffee and run to work. No time for the elevator today. I've got a job to do.

I finally get to the office. I take the stairs and run past Marge. I give her a wave. "Hey Marge!"

"Woo hoo! Sexy Mama!" she calls after me.

"You know it! Hey, is Ben in his office?" I ask.

"Nope. He has a few meetings this morning. Girl, don't get too hung up on him. He's a great boss, but he is a player," Marge says as she files her hot pink nails.

"Marge, he is so cute and so nice. He buys me presents and pays for dinner. He doesn't seem like a player to me. He came to bring me soup when I was sick."

"Girl, you are just a pawn in his game. You are falling for everything he throws at you. You have to give him a run for his money. Make him work, girl. Don't you go getting yourself into any trouble."

"I am very tough, Marge. Look at this finger." I show her the purity ring on my left hand.

"What is that?"

"When I turned 16, my dad bought me a purity ring to promise to save myself for marriage. I'm good. Promise."

"Well, I'm just telling you to be careful."

"Oh, Marge! Ben is too nice. He wouldn't try anything. Most guys try things on date number one. Ben is too sweet. He cares about me."

"Okay, alright! I've gotta get back to work. Good luck on party planning, Sweets."

"Thanks Marge." I walk to my office and open the door, spray perfume to cover the city smell off me, and get busy. I order the cake first. I don't want to make that mistake again. It's going to be a pretty castle cake. The baker said that the icing will be glittery. I didn't even know they made more than one kind of icing. I thought you could only have white or chocolate. Now they make glittery icing. Interesting.

This party is easier than the pyramid one. I don't have to send out invites and I don't have to get a caterer. I do, however, need to find a singer. I'm pretty sure 7 year olds listen to Miley Cyrus, Selena Gomez, and Disney people like that. I look online to find popular music groups for kids and I think I found a winner. I call the number listed and use Ben's name a lot to get connected through. I don't know if they can even do it, but I'll try my best. I beg, I plead, I even threaten to move the party to Universal Studios. I finally get a yes. Storm is going to have the cast of High School Musical and Miley Cyrus perform at her birthday party. I'm so good, I scare myself. I should wear this outfit more often!

After annoying Disney, I went to lunch. I didn't realize how long I had been on the phone. My arm kills and my brain hurts from jumping through the business hoops. I'm going to buy a headset before I come back. I run to McDonald's for lunch. I get a Big Mac and sit far away from the play area. I listen to my iPod while I eat. I hate eating alone. Here I am in my best outfit and I feel like a loser.

I stop by an electronic store and buy a headset for my office phone. As I walk back to work, I realize that I need luggage. I wonder if Mom used all of theirs. I think I'll go over there after work.

When I get back to the office, I attach the headset and call Disney World. I love that I can do that. I hold the power to call Disney World. I arrange for all of the Princesses to be at her party for the entire time. They remind me that the cost is going to be outrageous and I remind them that the parents don't care.

I also need to ask about the fireworks. I dial another number. "Hello. This is Maggie. May I help you?" she asks in her best cheerful Disney voice.

"Yes. I need to arrange for a fireworks display," I say in my professional voice.

"We don't do that," she says in the same cheery tone.

Crap! "Well, see, I'm planning a party and her parents want fireworks," I say.

"Well, can I give you some advice?" she asks again in the Disney voice. How can they talk like that all day? There must be some sort of phone voice training to work there.

"Sure," I say.

"Magic Kingdom does fireworks every night. Why don't you tell your clients that and let them know that Disney loves all little boys and girls, but they cannot do a special show. Hopefully, they will understand."

"Fantastic. I love you, Ms. Magic Kingdom!" I exclaim.

"My name is Maggie," she says.

"Sorry! I love you, Maggie. You are the most helpful person that I've talked to all day. Thank you!"

"No problem. Have a Disney day!"

I hang up and call it a day. It's only 4:00, but I'm caught up for now. I play around on Pinterest until 5:00. I tell Marge bye and I take a cab to my parents' house.

Gerta opens the door buck naked! Oh my gosh! "Gutentag!" she exclaims. I cover my eyes to the old, naked, German lady.

"Gerta! You are naked!" I yell.

"Sorry! My husband is home from work. We are celebrating his promotion," she says as she puts on her robe. Gross! Gross, flabby, German lady. I try to erase the image from my mind. Every time I close my eyes, she's there! Ewwww!

"Gerta, did my mom use all her luggage?" I ask.

"No. She took all of zee Louis Vuitton, but she left zee Gucci," she said.

"Thanks. I'll get it myself. You can go."

I go to the basement and rummage through everything until I find three pieces of Gucci luggage. I take it all to the cab and get the heck out of there. I do not ever want to see Gerta again. I can't believe that just happened. That would not happen to any other person. Only I could open the door to my parents' house and find the maid naked. Only me.

When I get home, Lynsey and Sam are cuddling on the couch and eating popcorn. I go into the kitchen and eat the leftover Chinese. I love old Chinese food. It is so much better the next day. I can't say it enough. As I finish off the last egg roll, I go into my bedroom to change into a black nightie. I put a robe on and go to the living room.

Sam and Lynsey are watching Legally Blonde. I curl up in the recliner and watch it with them. I love Reese Witherspoon. She is my hero. I mean she is pretty, nice, and professional. I decide to text Ben. "Hey babe!"

I wait for a reply. "Hey," he writes back.

"Want to come over?"

"Sorry. Can't. I'm in Jersey. Business Dinner," he texts.

"Oh, sorry. Bye." Crap! I'm so bored. I flip my Sidekick shut and walk to my bedroom. One more day of work before I can pack. I guess I'll just sleep. I thank God for loving me and creating cake! Amen!

I woke up this morning and felt someone sitting on the bed. I turn around and Ben is sitting on my bed holding coffee and donuts. "Hey! What a nice surprise!" I sit up and take the coffee and eat a donut.

"I thought I would surprise you. I know you missed me last night. I had a business dinner. I hired someone new. They needed to be welcomed."

"Oh." I am hoping that they were not welcomed like I was. "Man or woman?" I ask in a sweet voice.

"A young guy. He lives in Jersey, but he's going to move here. Don't worry, Cutie. I didn't buy him jewelry." He gives me a Crest smile.

"Good. We need new planners." I get out of bed and put my robe on quickly. "I'm almost finished with the party. All I have to do is reserve the restaurant for 200 people."

"Great! Get dressed and I'll drive you to work."

"Okay!" I run to the bathroom and shower. I flat iron my hair and put on shorts and an orange tank top. I slip on flip-flops and we leave.

We take the elevator and James looks surprised. "Hey, James! This is Ben, my boss slash boyfriend," I say as we get in. I sit on my bench that James warmed for me. Ben and James are looking at each other. I feel tension. Like a Lex and Superman tension. "Hi, Ben Sparks," James says.

"Hi, James Madden," Ben says.

Weird! They know each other. What is going on? Maybe they are Lex and Superman. Well, except James isn't bald. The doors part and Ben grabs me by the hand and pulls me to his car.

"How do you know him?" he asks me in an angry tone.

"He lives here! I wouldn't get so angry. He wants me to plan a party for him. This could be good money for us," I say.

"Babe, do you have any idea who he is?"

"No."

"That's James Madden. As in Madden Party Co. He is my biggest competition! (They are like Superman and Lex Luther. Cool!) He wants you. He found out about your Egyptian party. He found out about Emeril and The Plain White Tees. He wants you to plan his party alright. He wants you to plan for him. You cannot speak to him!" he shouts.

"I can't be rude. He hasn't asked me to work for him. I would never leave your company. Its okay, Baby. Calm down."

"Let's just go to work. Promise me that you will never speak to him again."

"I can't. I can't be rude, but I do promise that I will not talk about parties or your company. I won't say anything about what we do. Okay?"

"Fine. Let's go. I have a billion people to call today."

We get out of his Porsche and walk up to the office. Marge gives me a look and I follow Ben into his office. "Hey. Are you okay?" I ask.

"I'm fine. I have worked really hard to be where I am. I will do anything to keep me on top. James wants to take me down and I won't allow it. I'm fine, I promise. Go plan." He kisses me and I skip to my office.

I find the number for Cinderella's Royal Table and dial.

"Hello. This is Mark. May I help you?"

"My name is L.K. London. I work for Mr. Ben Sparks in New York. I need to reserve the place for 200 people. It's a birthday party and they want to have dinner there," I say.

"Um, for what day?" he asks.

"Next Friday night."

"That's really soon. I don't know if any openings. We usually need people to reserve 180 days in advance."

"180 days! These people just hired us a week ago. Oh, please see what you can do. They can pay more than whoever has the reservations now," I say hoping that the family doesn't want to kill me for spending all their money. Maybe they won't.

"I'll call the party and see if they can move it, but you will have to pay more. Give me your number and I'll call you back Ms. London."

I give him my number and wait for the call. I call Sam on my cell while I wait. "Sam, what's up?"

"Work. Are you ready to pack tomorrow? I am helping Lynsey so I can help you too. Is that cool?"

"Of course! I'll need some help deciding what to wear. Are you excited?"

"Yes! I'm already packed. I couldn't help it."

"I know. It's so cool that I get to take my friends with me to work in Florida. Hey, I need to talk to you later, okay?"

"Sure. L.K., I have to go. My boss is looking at me. Bye!"

"Bye!" As soon as I flipped my phone shut, my office phone rings. "Party Central. Ms. London speaking."

"Ms. London, this is Mark. I can fit your group in, but it is going to cost your clients big. I had to beg these old people to move their anniversary dinner to Saturday."

"Oh, thank you so much. When I get there, you are getting a hug."

"Great! I put my job on the line for a hug from a stranger."

"You will get a big tip too. Thank you, Mark!" I hang up and do a little dance. "I'm awesome! Go L.K.! Go L.K.!" The cabbage patch dance will never grow old.

I went through my checklist. Crap! I forgot to order gift bags. I order big pink Disney Princess bags filled with a Cinderella DVD, a princess charm bracelet, a tiara, princess stickers, princess bracelets, princess necklaces, and princess hair stuff, and anything else with princesses on them. I order 200 of everything and get them shipped to my office ASAP! I had to skip lunch in order to finish making the bags. I get them shipped to our suite in Orlando. I call the manager to let them know to hold them until we get there Friday night. He was really nice about it.

At 5:30, I finally get to go home. I want to eat and shower. I walk home and get in the elevator. I can't walk anymore. My feet are killing me! The doors part and James is looking right at me. I think he lives in the elevator. I don't think he really has an apartment. I wave at him and get in. "Hey!" I say.

"Well, hello. I guess you know who I am now," he says.

"You could have told me. Ben totally freaked out on me this morning."

"Sorry. After you told me that you worked for him, I thought that I should just keep my mouth shut."

"I guess."

"You know if anything happens, you can come work for me."

"Oh, don't go there. This is what Ben said you would say. I appreciate the offer, but I can't betray him. He is my boyfriend."

"Be careful with him. In the business, you hear things."

"Okay. That's it! I'm so tired of everyone telling me to be careful. I am an adult, you know. I can make my own decisions. Thank you for your input, but I am not a child and I'll date who I want to date!" The doors part. Finally! I stomp out of the elevator leaving James speechless and into my apartment. Maybe I went a little crazy for a moment, but I needed to throw a mini fit. Everyone gets one of those every once in a while, right?

Lynsey comes up to me, "L.K., I'm so excited. I can't wait! Thank you so much for inviting me. Hey, are you okay? You're face is really red."

"I'm fine. I just yelled at a guy in the elevator, so I'm good now. Have you packed yet?" I ask.

"Nope. I'm waiting until tomorrow. Hey, we are going to 21 Club tonight. Do you want to come with us?" she asks.

"Nah, I'm going to call Ben. I want to talk him into coming to see me," I say.

"He works a lot, huh?" she asks.

"Yeah, but we get to see each other every day next week. I'm so ready for that," I say.

"I bet. Hey, can I ask you a question?" she asks.

"Sure. What's up?" I ask.

"Are you avoiding spending time with me and Sam? I mean, anytime that we are together, you find a way to disappear," she says.

"Oh, no, I'm not avoiding you. I just don't want to be in the way." Not! I hate being around you two together. "I've just been really busy. I'm sorry if you thought I was avoiding you guys. Hey, we'll talk later. I just want to relax. I'm going to take a long bath. Okay?"

"Okay, I'm glad that you are not mad about me and Sam," she says.

I walk into my bedroom and strip! July is not my friend. My pits are sweating and I smell. I think I'll take a long, bubble bath. I start the water and hop in. I'm going to stay in here until my skin is wrinkled. I tried to call Sam, but I got no answer. I guess I'll have to talk to him later. He probably left his phone on silent again. Oh well.

After my bath, I put on a red nightie and I slip under the covers. I watch Grey's Anatomy and balance my checkbook. I'm not very good at remembering to write down what I spend with my debit card. I've got to get better at that. I'm so exhausted. Throwing fits and planning parties can really take it out of you. I'm going to sleep. I pray and I lock my bedroom door. No one is going to wake me up until I'm ready. I switch the light off and I'm out.

Chapter 11

When I finally wake up, I look at my clock. 2:00 p.m.! That means that I've been sleeping since...11:00 p.m. I shouldn't have to sleep for days! I can't believe that I have been asleep that long. I wonder why no one has called or beat on my door. Strange. I walk into the kitchen and no one is here. Strange. I go into Lynsey's room. No one. I am in my apartment alone. Very Strange.

I check the messages. "L.K., this is Sam. I can't find Lynsey. We were supposed to meet at 21 Club and she never showed. I was wondering if you could call me if you hear from her. Bye." Strange.

It's like she disappeared. Maybe she was abducted by aliens. Okay, I've been watching Signs way too much.

I call her cell and she doesn't answer. I have no idea what is going on. She better show up. We leave tomorrow. I look in her room again. She is already packed. I thought she said she was going to wait until today? Strange.

I decide to call Sam. I'm starting to get worried. "Sam, have you talked to Lynsey yet?"

"No. I have looked everywhere for her. Her parents are out of town and she wasn't at the apartment. I don't know what to do."

"Come over. Maybe she'll show up soon. Okay?"

"Okay."

I shut my phone and I make a pot of coffee. I decide to order pizza while I wait on Sam.

"Pete's Pizza, this is Joey," he says. Why is it that I never get to speak with Pete? It's a Mystery.

"I would like to order two large pizzas with the works. I'll need cheesy bread too. Heck, why not, throw in three salads with ranch."

"Will that be all?"

"Um, pie. We need pie. What cha got?"

"Coconut, chocolate, and I think we have a cheesecake too."

"Cheesecake. That will be all," I tell him my address and I pay with a credit card. I'll need all of my cash for the trip.

Sam walks in wearing an old, ratty, Charlie Brown t-shirt and ripped jeans. He looks tired. "Sam, it's time that the shirt goes. It has holes in the armpits. That's not exactly the way to attract the ladies."

"I love this shirt."

"Linus, let the blanket go!"

"Maybe later. Have you heard anything yet?"

"Nope. I ordered food though."

"I'm starving."

"You look tired too."

"I didn't sleep. I looked for Lynsey all night. I went everywhere. I couldn't sleep because I was so worried. What if someone got her? What if..."

"Sam, I think she's fine. I'm sure there's a reasonable explanation why she's not here. Calm down. Why don't you go to my room and sleep? I'll stay by the phone."

"Ok." He gives me a huge hug. "You are the greatest friend."

"I know. Now, go sleep. I'll wake you up when the food gets here." He walks to my bedroom and shuts the door. Poor Sam. Lynsey better have a good excuse. I'd hate to have to kick her out.

The pizza guy finally shows up and there is still no word from Lynsey. I tip the pizza boy and I put everything on the counter. I wake Sam and we eat. He eats a whole pizza by himself. He really was starving. I can't believe all of this drama with Lynsey. Its 4:00 already and I haven't packed.

I put in Die Hard to help cheer up Sam so we flop on the couch. I prop Sam's head on a pillow in my lap and we watch Bruce Willis be a hero. He finally falls asleep and I start to read Twilight where I left off. The phone rings and we both jump. I answer, "Hello. Lynsey?"

"Nope. Ben. You're looking for Lynsey?"

"Yeah, she was supposed to meet Sam at 21 Club last night, but she never showed."

"That's weird. I had a business dinner at Jean George's last night on the Upper West Side and I saw her having dinner with some guy. I thought it was Sam."

"She was having dinner? Strange."

"Well, I was calling to tell you that I'll be at your apartment with a Limo at 11:30 a.m. tomorrow. Make sure everyone is ready."

"Hey, did you say you had a business dinner last night?"

"Yep. I had dinner with bank people. I need a loan to buy the building next door," he says.

"Another building? Cool. We're adding on? That's great!"

"Well, I have to have another dinner tonight to settle the deal. I may stop by after dinner, but don't wait up for me. Catch ya later, Babe."

"Bye!" I look at Sam and I don't know what to say. He is looking at me. "Uh, Sam, that was Ben."

"She had dinner, huh?" He looks so sad.

"Yep." I don't want to tell him it was with a guy. He is going to be crushed. Before I have the chance to tell him, I hear the lock turn. Lynsey skips in holding a million shopping bags. I can't believe her! Sam has been so worried and she went shopping. Mall Tramp! Sam walks up to her. Oh, no, this is going to be bad. I better get popcorn!

"Lynsey, where have you been?" he shouts.

"Shopping. Why are you screaming?" she asks.

"Lynsey, I looked all over for you last night. You want to tell me about this dinner you had?"

"Sam, I left you three messages. One on your cell and two at your house."

"I haven't been home. I've been looking for you. Tell me about this dinner."

"Sam, calm down. My old friend, Adam, from Dallas came in to see me. I couldn't turn him down. He was only here for one night."

"Oh, a he, an Adam! Great! You could have invited him to eat with us and why haven't you answered your cell?"

"Sam, my battery died. You have got to calm down. Anyway, you shouldn't get angry with me about Adam. You eat with L.K. all of the time without me. I don't get jealous or angry. I know that you two are friends. I'm sorry. I got excited when he called and I just didn't think. I'm sorry. Don't be mad. I said I was super sorry. It was just a big misunderstanding." She grabs him and kisses him. Yuck! I was kind of hoping that we would get to kick her out. Crap!

They went into her bedroom. Crap again! Now they are going to make out and I have to pack by myself.

I change into sweats and begin packing. I turn on Gilmore Girls to give me motivation. Loralei Gilmore always gets me feeling good again. We share a name. I end up using all three Gucci suitcases and three of my own. One for shoes, one for hair and make-up stuff, one for shirts, one for shorts/pants, one for dresses, and one for night stuff and everything else. Crap! I need a carry on. I find a huge Louis Vuitton purse and use that. I put snacks, books, plane tickets, and my camera in the bag. I'm set! I'm ready! Florida here I come!

I hear a knock at my door. "Come in!" It's Sam. He looks happy. I finally notice that he got his hair cut. Good! I couldn't take the Sebastian Bach look anymore. "Hey, you. How'd it go?"

"Good. Lynsey explained everything."

"I think that she should've waited until you showed up. She can't just disappear like that."

"Oh, well. It's in the past. I see you packed. You have seven bags! Did you pack everything?"

"No." He looks in my walk-in closet and shakes his head.

"You have way too many clothes. What are you going to wear on the plane?"

"I figured that I would go with my stretchy jeans and my shirt that says, "Edward Cullen is my Valentine."

"Who is this Edward Cullen? I see his name everywhere."

"He is the one of the main characters in the Twilight Series. He's the hot vampire that is love with a human."

"So, you are saying that you are going to wear a shirt that says your valentine is a vampire character in a book?" he asks.

"Yeah. So?"

"First of all, it's July. It's not February. Secondly, it's a character."

"The character is romantic and the actor that plays him in the movie is super hot!" I say.

"Okay, whatever. I'm not having a conversation about a book character. At least wear your Elvis pajamas."

"Not on the plane. I brought them though. So, everything is okay with you and Lynsey?"

"Yeah, we're good. It was just a misunderstanding. You want to come watch Friends? Mrs. Tragger is here. She said that you forgot about her and she brought her DVD set. She said you owe her two hours of Friends since you forgot to come over."

"Oh, snaps! I did forget." We walk into the living room and Mrs. Tragger is wearing her Friends pajamas and tells me to change into mine. She bought them for me last Christmas.

I change and I go back in the living room. "Okay! I'm changed. Let's watch Friends."

"You forgot. I can't believe you forgot. Make some popcorn, Missy!" she yells from the couch.

"All right, Hildie May, you better watch your 'tude. I'll kick you out."

"Lora Kate, you don't want me to put the hurt on you. I do Pilates."

"I didn't think people your age could do Pilates."

"Watch it. You're not too big for a whippin'. I'll take a belt to that scrawny behind."

I laugh and plop down beside her. Sam and Lynsey are cuddled on the recliner. We all watch Friends in peace. It's interesting how a show about a group of six people who spend most of their time in a coffee house can bring peace to our group. I'm even sitting in the same room as the lovebirds. We eat the rest of the pizza and devour the cheesecake.

I look over by the door and see luggage. "Sam, did you bring your luggage over here?"

"Yep! I'm sleeping on the couch. I'm not going to oversleep this time."

"We're not leaving until 11:30."

"So. I sleep until 1:00 and from the looks of you earlier, you do too."

"Fine, but do not wear that shirt on the plane?"

"I think it's cute," Lynsey says. What does she know? She doesn't realize that he wears that shirt twice a week, every week.

"Well, I think it's gross. It had holes in the pits," I say.

"How's this for holes in the pits?" he asks with a smile as comes over and puts his pits over my face.

I kick him and he grabs my foot. "Let go!" I scream. Lynsey gives me a look and I pull away. Woah, what's your damage, Heather? I think I'm going to stay on my side of the world from now on.

"Just for that, I'm wearing this outfit on the plane. I'm not even going to shower," he says as he sniffs his armpits.

"Gross!" I look over at Mrs. Tragger. She is asleep. I wake her up and walk her home.

When I walk back into my apartment, I see Ben sitting on the couch. I run to him and sit on his lap. He kisses me and holds me for a long time. "I am so glad that you are here. I feel like we haven't seen each other in a month," I say.

"I know, Baby. I have to work. Good news though, I got the loan. Construction starts as soon as we leave. I'll be able to hire 50 more people. It's all about the Benjamins, Baby!" he exclaims. Okay, he does not need to sing Diddy songs for me to get the point, but he's so cute.

I kiss him and fill him in on all of the drama. "Hey, I bought something for you to wear on the plane," he says.

"What?" He buys me a lot of things. I love it! He hands me a bag. I look in and pull out a little lacy dress with no back. Whoa! A little slutty for me. What should I say? I can't say that I love it and I cannot wear that on the plane. "Um, thanks, Baby."

"Florida will be hot. I want you to be comfortable," he says.

Comfortable! It's a dress! I'm going to look like I belong on the street corner! I'll be Julia Roberts in Pretty Woman! "Great! Thanks!" I shove the dress back in the bag and kiss him. I'll just have to wear a sweater. I'm going to burn up.

"Well, Sweetie, I have to go. I want to get plenty of sleep. I'll see you in the morning!" He gives me a deep kiss and leaves.

I pull the dress back out the minute Sam walks in from Lynsey's room. "What is that? A scarf?" he asks.

"Nope, it's a dress. A dress that I have to wear on the plane, because Ben wants me to be comfortable in hot Florida," I say with a face.

"Well, try it on. See if it fits. If it doesn't, then tell him it didn't fit and don't wear it."

"Great idea!" I run to the bedroom and put it on. Crap! It fits. I walk out and Sam's eyes get wide. "What?" I ask.

"Nothing. It fits. Wow!"

"Stop it! I feel very cheap right now! It fits. What am I going to do? I can't wear this. God will punish me if I wear this. It's too revealing." I look in the mirror. Crap! Not only is the back cut out, you can see my entire stomach through the lace. I cannot wear this.

"Just tell him it didn't fit. I think it would be okay to lie in this case."

"Yeah, I guess. I don't like to lie, but I definitely don't want to hurt his feelings and I just can't wear this in public. They might "randomly" search me in the airport for looking conspicuous." I really don't like to lie, but it seems that I've been doing it a lot lately. At that moment, Lynsey walks in.

"Wow, are we giving a show?" she asks as she looks at me in the slut dress and gives me that look again.

"Um, not really. This is a present from Ben. It is what I'm supposed to wear on the plane," I say.

"I say lie," Sam says.

"Me too," Lynsey agrees.

"Okay. I'll lie, but I'm not going to enjoy it." With that I get back into my pajamas and I hide the dress in the back of my closet. Maybe I'll use it as a gag gift one day. I get into bed and pray for a safe trip and the designer of the hideous dress. Amen!

Chapter 12

I wake up at 7:00 and look over toward my bathroom. And who do I see? Sam! Sitting on my toilet reading Cosmopolitan! "Sam! Learn to close the door!" I run over and shut the door. How nasty! I hear him giggle! "Sam! That is disgusting! I did not want the first thing I see to be you on the toilet!"

"Sorry! I figured you were out cold! I hate to close the bathroom door. I'm claustrophobic! You know that!" he yells.

"You are not that claustrophobic and don't talk to me while you're in there! Gross!" I hear the toilet flush and he opens the door with a smile. I punch him in the stomach and he throws me on the bed and tickles me! "Stop! I have to pee!" I yell. I jump off the bed and run into the bathroom and lock the door. It smells nasty in here.

I Febreeze the nasty out of the bathroom and get ready. As soon as I dress in my original plane outfit, I go into the kitchen where Lynsey is making breakfast.

"Good morning, L.K.!" Lynsey says in a cheery voice.

"Morning, roomie!" I grab a cup of coffee and plop down beside Sam. Lynsey is making pancakes! I love pancakes and her pancakes are so fluffy!

I run over and turn on the T.V. I change the channel and find Full House. It doesn't matter what time of day you want to watch T.V., Full House will be on somewhere. It's a conspiracy from the government to make all families end their troubles in thirty minutes or less.

We eat breakfast and watch four episodes of the Tanner Family. They get along way too well for a family with one parent and two other guys living in the same house. You have to admit though, that those Olsen twins are quite cute.

It seems like time is passing so slow. It's only 10:30. We don't leave for another hour. Our luggage is waiting by the door. I decide to add another book to my carry on. I look on the bookshelf and decide to bring the whole Twilight series for the flight. I stick it them in my carry on. I have seven bags and Lynsey and Sam have two each. I feel silly, but I can't condense anything. I need it all. I get that from my mother. I wonder what she is buying me from Rome. Probably a key chain.

11:30 finally arrives and we load everything into the Limo. Ben looks at me. Crap! I have to lie. I'm not a very good liar. "Hey, Baby!" I kiss him to soften the look.

"Where's your new dress? I spent a fortune on that dress for you to wear on the plane," he says. Oh, no. He's mad.

"It didn't fit. I tried it on last night and my thighs were popping out of the lace. I didn't want to embarrass you," I say in a sweet, sexy voice.

"Huh, I could have sworn that I got the right size. Well, take it back and get another one in your size. You can wear it for me when we get back," he says.

Oh great! I have to wear that thing for him. I feel like a dog that people dress. I hate that! When you see Paris Hilton in magazines, she always has that Chihuahua dressed up to match her.

It's awful! You can tell he's embarrassed. Sam and Lynsey are smiling. I hope Ben's not too mad. I absolutely cannot wear that thing.

When we got to the airport, we got searched and our luggage was searched. No wonder Ben said we should leave early. We finally got on the airplane. I always hate this part. The waiting. I always feel like they make us wait to fix something that is wrong. They shouldn't board you if they are not ready to leave. It's ridiculous! I always have that weird feeling in my stomach that we are going to end up on an island like Tom Hanks talking to a volleyball or like those people who ended up on that island with polar bears. I've gotta shake it off! It's not like Final Destination or anything. Is it?

We are flying first class and man, is it fancy! I am sitting between Ben and Sam, which kind of feels weird. Their male egos are about to squish me. The stewardess walks past and I stop her. "What movie are we watching today?"

"It can either be Music Man or Sound of Music. You choose," she says.

Old school stuff, hmm…..what to choose? What to choose? I feel privileged. "Um, how about Music Man?" I ask.

"Sounds great. You just made my job easier. Thanks." She walks away and I smile. I could be a flight attendant. Didn't Gwyneth Paltrow play a flight attendant in some movie? If she can do it, I know I can. I have people skills, but then again, my chances of dying in an airplane would get higher so never mind.

The plane finally takes off and Ms. Plane Lady starts the movie. As soon as we find out that there is trouble in River City, the seat belt sign turns off.

I get up and go to the bathroom. When I come back, Sam and Lynsey are making out and Ben is giving me a look. I'm guessing that he wants to make out too. I have to say that a make out contest is not my idea of a fun plane ride. People are staring and there are kids running around kicking on peoples' seats. Besides, Music Man is on and I love this movie.

I squeeze past Sam and Lynsey and sit beside Ben. He kisses me on the neck and I kiss him back. "Hey, can I tell you something?" I ask.

"Sure," Ben says.

"Do you really like me?" I ask.

"Of course. Why?" he asks.

"Well, you have that look on your face that says that you want to make out and I really love The Music Man. If you really like me, you'll let me watch one of my favorite musicals. Could we kiss later? I don't feel comfortable kissing on a plane. I feel like all of the children are looking at me and I'm afraid that the parents will begin to get angry. I really like my seat and I don't want to be thrown out by the nice plane people. Is that okay?" I ask with a pout.

"Sure. I want you to feel comfortable," he says even though he didn't sound very convincing.

"Good." With that, I felt better. I watched the movie in peace and then fell asleep.

When I wake up, we are in Orlando. Hello, Florida! I realize that everyone else is awake and staring at me. "What?"

Ben leans over and whispers, "Your shirt is kind of twisted."

Crap! I look down and see that my shirt is twisted up by my bra and you can see all the pretty lace. I don't even know how that happened. I don't think I could even move around like that in this chair even though I am known as a very restless sleeper at times. I can wake up in the morning and all of the covers are on the floor. I blame Ben or one of those little nasty kids that was running up and down the hallway. I pull my shirt down and we leave the plane with every parent giving me dirty looks.

We walk into a crowded Orlando airport. It's beautiful! Everyone is wearing floral shirts. Old men are in flowery shorts and big hats. I love it!

We get our bags and find our Limo waiting. I love riding in a Limo. It makes me feel rich and famous. Mr. Airport Man takes our luggage and loads it in the trunk. "How many bags did you bring, L.K.?" Ben asks.

"Seven, but I need them all. I can't help it," I say.

"Sure," he says with a smile.

The driver takes us to the land of Mickey Mouse. I stick my head out of the sunroof and enjoy the view. Florida is so beautiful! Sam comes up with me and we both admire all that is Disney.

We stop as soon as we reach Animal Kingdom Lodge. It's very cool, but I can smell the animals. I think that I'm going to enjoy this week even though I have to work. I jump out of the Limo spin around. I am in paradise! Ben grabs me and kisses me. "We are going to have a beautiful week, Baby," he says as he picks me up and carries me into the suite. Sam and Lynsey follow us.

The suite is awesome! Lynsey and I go to our room and fall on the beds. "I can't believe we are finally here."

"I know. It's great! Hey, how do you think Ben and Sam will get along?" she asks as she sits up.

"I don't know. I hope they will be fine. They only have to sleep there. Guys!"

"I know! They are so incompetent!" she says as she giggles. "Yeah, they think staying in a room together is weird. Like people will talk. It's not like they're those two magicians from Vegas with the tigers."

She says, "I know!"

I turn on the T.V. There is something about watching television in your hotel room that is better than home. I don't know. There's just something cool about it like all the good stuff only comes on when you are on vacation in a hotel.

We spend the rest of the night in our rooms. It's too late to do anything else. We order room service and play Phase 10.

"I hate this game!" Sam yells.

"You only hate it because you're losing," I say.

Lynsey says, "I don't think I get it yet."

"Me either. You want to watch T.V. while they finish?" Ben asks.

"Sure," she says. Weird. I don't know why, but weird! It's not a hard game like chess.

Sam and I finish the game and join them. They are watching CSI. I hate this show. Sam always figures the mystery out and I never get it until it is pointed out to me directly at the end. Ben and Lynsey are on the same couch so Sam and I sit on another one. So Weird.

I kiss Ben goodnight and I go to my room. Lynsey follows. We put on our pajamas and get into bed. Big day tomorrow. I tell God goodnight and I watch T.V. I can't sleep so I watch Food Network. I love to watch other people cook. I can't do it, but its fun to watch.

I look over at Lynsey and she is watching too. "Can't sleep?" I ask.

"Nope."

"You like Iron Chef?"

"Yep."

"Cool." We watch it together in silence. I finally turn it to Lifetime. That will definitely put us to sleep. I know they play good movies, but you can begin watching it and turn it off. Then, when you turn it back on hours later, they are still playing the same kind of movie so you get confused. We finally fall asleep to an insipid movie about a girl who overcomes some trial. Big surprise!

I wake up to the smell of bacon. Is Lynsey already up? We didn't get to sleep until 3:00 a.m. I look over and she is still asleep. Oh well, I decide to sleep. I'll eat later. I'm too tired.

Not 30 minutes later, I hear a knock at the door. I growl and ignore it. I'm so tired. The knock comes again. No! No! No! I'm not getting up. I am going to sleep until I'm tired again.

"Is that you?" Lynsey asks.

"No, someone is knocking," I say.

"Do you think if we ignore it, it will go away?"

"Not likely." I stand up and open the door to Ben. He is wide-eyed and bushy tailed and he is wearing shorts! I have never seen him in anything but suits. He even wore one on the plane.

"Hey, Honey. Time to get up and get ready," he says.

"Why?" I ask.

"We have a whole day. We are going to enjoy our day by visiting Animal Kingdom. Then, we are going to drive to Universal and eat dinner at City Walk and go dancing," he says with a smile.

"You have planned the whole day before 9:00 a.m. How long have you been up?" I ask.

"Well, I got up at 5:00 a.m. and took a jog. I made breakfast for everyone, which is on the table. I read the paper and unpacked everything in the closet and drawers," he says.

"You had a whole day before I got up," I say.

Ben kisses me and looks over at Lynsey who has fallen asleep again. "I'm guessing that you girls stayed up too late, huh?"

"We couldn't sleep. I'll be out in a bit. Okay?"

"Okay, Baby. Hurry and tell Lynsey to get up too. I want us all to stay together," he says.

"Is Sam up?" I ask.

"I woke him up this morning. He is watching cartoons, I believe. See you in a bit," he says as he closes the door. I lock it and wake Lynsey up.

We take turns in the bathroom and get dressed. I wear khaki shorts and a red tank top with Mickey Mouse on the front. Showing a little Disney love! I put my hair into pigtails to add to the Minnie Mouse look. I skip out of my room and find breakfast. Bacon, eggs, and pancakes. Yummy! I look out the window and see giraffes. Giraffes! I love this job!

I look over at Sam and he is laughing. "What, Loser!" I yell I can't stand that. He is always laughing at me. It's not fair.

"You look like a member of the Mickey Mouse Club. Cute, real cute," he says.

"And you look like a member of N'SYNC. I am sporting the Mouse look, yes, but I'm doing it for the good of all things Disney," I say in my most professional voice.

"Come watch TV, Ms. Disney."

I grab some breakfast and walk over to sit beside him. He flips my pigtails and smiles at me. I roll my eyes. What is taking Lynsey so long? I'm ready to go. I want to see all of Orlando. Well, at least all of Disney World.

Lynsey finally emerges from our room. She is dressed in a mini skirt and a tube top. Her blonde hair is curled and bouncy. Who is she trying to impress? I have never seen her dress like that in all our roomie days. Strange. This trip is just weird. I look over at Sam and he is drooling. Gross! I take a napkin and wipe his face. "Sam, you are drooling."

"Oh, sorry." He stands and walks toward Lynsey. "Hey, Babe! Nice outfit!"

"Thanks. It's so hot outside. I wanted to dress cool," she says. Whatever! She is dressing to impress. I'm a woman too and no one dresses like that unless they are trying to get all the attention. I don't know what is going on, but I will get to the bottom of this.

My thoughts are interrupted by Ben. "Is everyone ready?" We all stand and follow him out. He is so sexy in those shorts! So Abercrombie! So Hot! As we walk out, Ben looks at Lynsey. "You look nice," he says. What about me? Do I not look nice? Well, this sucks! Crap!

"Thanks. I thought I would dress cool. I used to live here. I know how to dress in this hot weather," she says. She has lived here before? I need to get to know my roommate. I know nothing about her. This sucks! I look at Sam. I try to send vibes to him to compliment me. He doesn't get them.

Sam says, "Lynsey, you do look hot and I'm lovin' it!" He kisses her. What am I, invisible? I have to do something.

"Well, I personally think that everyone looks nice today," I say hoping for some agreement. Everyone nods. Crap! I'm nonexistent!

We walk to the park. I walk really close to Ben. I grab his hand and he kisses it. Why is everyone quiet? I can't take it. I feel like screaming. Ben looks like a man on a mission. Sam is drooling over Lynsey and she is looking hot apparently. I hate this. Crap!

Before I get the chance to scream in annoyance, we enter the park. I grab a park map. I open it up and look at all of the pictures. I don't know how to read this. "It looks all jumbled to me. I don't know how to read it!" I feel frustrated. I feel like running to the airport and catch the next ticket back to NYC!

"Here. Gimme," Sam says as he snatches it from me. He looks at it and points to the right. "I want to go there." Sam pointed to the Kilimanjaro Safari. We began walking over when I tripped and fell flat on my face. Crap!

"Lora Kate London starring in Swan Lake!" Sam said with a laugh.

I pull myself up and said, "You don't have to be so rude. You could've helped me up. You know, I'm getting sick of you always laughing at me."

"I know, but it's always fun to laugh at you," he says.

"Gee, thanks." Ben kisses me and we all march over to go on the safari. Yay, animals. I'm not exactly thrilled about being here right now. I guess I should try to have a better attitude. Maybe. It's amazing how one morning can turn my entire attitude from great to sour. We all climb into a Jeep and take off. Okay, this is pretty awesome with all of the exotic animals! The Jeep stops when we reach a beautiful giraffe. He walks over to us and I can't help it. I know that we are not supposed to touch the animals, but I can't help it. I reach out and touch his leg. The giraffe reaches down and I stroke his head. He is so soft. It's like Lion King, but real. I want a giraffe.

When the safari comes to an end, we decide to ride the Kali River Rapids, It's Tough to be a Bug, and Dinosaur, which, by the way, scared me half to death. I thought the dinosaurs were real. No one said Jurassic Park wasn't real. Those Disney people could have had real dinosaurs made. You never can tell what rich people will do for entertainment. That Walt Disney is sneaky. I mean, they can make icing glittery. If they can do that, they can do anything. Who knows?

I really want to eat. We skipped lunch so we could ride all of the rides. It's getting kind of late and I'm starving. I rub my growling stomach.

"Honey, we are going to eat at Universal tonight," Ben says as he kisses my sweaty forehead.

"I know, but I'm starving. All of that dinosaur drama got me all worked up," I say as I lead everyone into the Rainforest Café. It's very cool in here. It's about time we found some air conditioning. I am about to die of a heat stroke. No one warned me that it was going to be 500 degrees here.

"L.K., what is this place?" Sam asks as we find a seat.

"I don't know. The Internet people said that this was a good place," I say.

"The Internet people?"

"Yes. I don't remember what site it was on, but they said it was good."

"Well, if the whole Internet agrees, then it must be the best," Sam says with a smile. He tosses my pigtails. "By the way, you look cute too." Thank You! Some recognition! Ben gives Sam a "back off" look and now I'm uncomfortable. Superman and Lex all over again.

"Hey, Baby, you do look adorable," Ben says as he kisses my neck. I feel very strange right now.

"Thanks!" I say as I try to make myself feel comfortable. Now Lynsey is giving me a look. Great! I wiggle my nose and try to make the moment disappear.

After our odd, but late lunch, we go back to the room to shower and change. I decide to wear my hot pink Barbie dress and heels. If we are going dancing, I want to look awesome. I twist my hair and wait in the living room while everyone gets ready. I flip on the T.V. and watch Veronica Mars. She makes me feel powerful. I need that.

Lynsey walks out in a red dress very similar to the one that I stuffed in the back of my closet. It's not quite as slutty, but it definitely has a slutty quality. What has gotten into her? It's vacation, not Spring Break. "Wow, you look....nice," I say with my best smile.

"Thanks," she says as she flips her hair.

Of course Sam was drooling and Ben said she looked nice too. I twirl around in front of Ben and Sam to get a few compliments.

"You look amazing, Baby. I see you are wearing my necklace," Ben says as he kisses me.

"Hey, Malibu Barbie!" Sam says with a giggle. Okay, I'm tired of this. He is really getting on my nerves with the comments. Lynsey looks great enough to drool over, but I get a Barbie remark. Yes, it is my Barbie dress, but I don't want to be called Barbie. Wait a minute! What am I so upset about? Ben thinks I look amazing. What do I care what Sam says?

"Thanks. I was going for the whole Barbie look!" I say.

We took a Limo to City Walk and walked into Emeril's restaurant. Ben had booked us reservations. I hope Emeril isn't here. He might remember our rendezvous in New York. It's so fancy. The host walks us to our table and gives us a menu. "Nice place, Baby," I say after the waiter takes our order.

"Anything for my love," he says as he kisses me. We haven't been seeing each other very long and he is really getting too close and calling me his love. Well, that's just strange. I have a feeling that this trip is going to be life changing.

After dinner we head out for dancing. I can't believe that this is our second night here. The club is hopping and we are having an amazing time. Ben reaches over and says, "Hey, I have to make some calls real quick. I'll be back." With that, he was gone and I'm in the middle of the dance floor alone. Well, I feel like a loser. The song (of course) changes to a slow one and I am alone. I go over beside Sam and Lynsey who are drinking water by the bar.

"Hey, someone dance with me. I feel like a loser," I say as I grab Sam's water.

"Well, it would be kind of strange for us to dance together," Lynsey says.

Sam jumps in, "I'll dance with you, Loser. That okay, Lynsey?"

"Sure," she says giving me that look again. Weird.

Sam and I travel to the dance floor. "So, how's your trip?" I ask.

"Great! I feel like something big is going to happen this week, don't you?" he asks as he puts his arms around my waist.

This feels different. Comfortable? Nah, just familiar. "Yeah, I do."

"Where did Ben get off to?"

"Making calls. He's a busy man," I say as I lean closer to Sam. It's really loud in here. I can barely hear him.

"I guess so. Lynsey said that you girls are going to talk tonight. Something about bonding."

"Yep! I need to get to know her better. I didn't even know that she used to live here. I guess I've been too busy being crazy about the two of you, which I'm totally fine with."

"I'm glad that you said that. She's really great, L.K and I have you to thank for bringing her into my life. She is like fresh air."

"I'm glad you're happy, Sam."

"Are you happy?"

"Yep!" I don't want to talk anymore. I do not want to hear about his happiness. I just feel like something is going to happen. Something bad. I can't shake this feeling that there is going to be some drama. I don't want drama. I want to enjoy my vacation.

Before the dance ends, Ben walks up to us. He cuts in and we finish the song. I want to go back to the room. I'm already tired and I have a night of talking to do. "Can we go back to the room?" I ask Ben.

"Sure," he says as he scoops me up.

All four of us leave the club and go back to the room to get comfy. I kiss Ben goodnight and go to my room. "Okay, let's get to talking," I say as I plop on the bed.

"Okay, tell me about you," Lynsey says.

"Okay, I'm 23. I grew up in New York and went to public school. I probably had way too many friends because my grades were pretty average. I always had a dog of some sort. One dog that we had, Boo Boo, I think secretly wanted to kick me out of the house. I'm an only child, which explains my need to have everything that I want, but my parents are two of the best people in the world. They always help me out when I need them and I have them to thank for teaching me to lead a Christian life. They are in Rome right now for the summer. Apparently, America is boring to them at the moment. They currently have a maid named Gerta who is staying at my parents' house while they are gone. Do not meet her. She is well, not modest. I went to NYU where I met Sam. I have been fired from many jobs and my last roommate moved out because she met her "soul mate" on the Internet. I like to read and watch movies. I absolutely love coffee and that's about it," I say. Wow, now that I have told her about my life, it seems kind of boring. "So…tell me about you."

Lynsey puts a pillow behind her head, "Well, where do I start? I was born in L.A., but my father said that he hated to live where celebrities show themselves, so we moved to Washington D.C. I finished elementary school there, but then my dad got transferred to Orlando. We lived here until I graduated high school. I have to say that I love Florida the most. I mean Florida has the sun, the beach, and the guys! (Okay, weird to me. Is it just me or is she a flirt?) As soon as I graduated, we all moved to New York. Dad loves it. He says that he loves to live in a place where the "freakin' sun doesn't shine all day!" I started NYU with a mind to get a degree in education, but then I realized that I hated children. I had no patience for wiping noses all day so I changed my major to business. In fact, I want to do party planning when I graduate, so I was surprised when I found out that you were a party planner. It was like fate or something. On that note, do you think Ben would give me an internship next semester?" she asks.

Okay, we are bonding not trying to get ahead in life, but I decide to say, "Sure, just ask him. I'm sure he would love to give you an internship." Why did I say that? I don't want her working with me. Then, Sam will be at my place of work all of the time kissing and making out with Lynsey. I don't know if I can take that. I don't know if I can handle that type of stress?

"Awesome!" she says. "That's about it. There's not much else to say. Ice cream?"

I say, "Sure! I never reject ice cream. Bring it on!" Okay, her life is better than mine. She dresses better than me. She has the same interests that I do. Why do I not just love her? What is wrong with me?

Lynsey finds the ice cream and we pig out and watch MTV's The Hills until we fall asleep. This has been quite a day. I have to say though that all I can think about is dancing with Sam. I know that he's my friend. He's my best friend, but when we were dancing, I felt so safe. I didn't really have to think about anything at all. It was kind of nice.

Chapter 13

I woke up this morning with Sam staring in my face. "What?" I groan as a pull the covers over my face.

"Get up! It's Sunday and it's 3:00 p.m.! What's wrong with you? You girls have to go to sleep earlier. You sleep like a bear," he says.

"3:00 p.m.! Sammy! Why didn't someone wake me up?"

"I tried and you pinched me!"

"I did not," I say as I sit up and look at his arm. "I did pinch you and really hard. Is that blood? Sorry."

"I just hope that I don't get a disease or something," he says as he pulls me out of bed by my feet.

"Whatever! I can't believe I slept that long. I guess I was exhausted and didn't realize it. Did anyone else try to wake me up?"

"Ben and Lynsey. Lynsey said that she shook you forever and you didn't wake up. She was afraid you were dead or something. Ben said that he kissed you and you still didn't wake up. I can't believe he thought giving you a Prince Charming kiss would wake you."

"What have I missed?"

"We went to Epcot this morning. I knew you wouldn't mind if you missed it. It's not the best park in Disney World. Well, I hope you didn't mind anyway."

"No, I don't care. I needed to rest before I start getting everything ready for that party. I have to wrap everything up this week. That party is going to be a hit! I've got to make sure the cake, the restaurant, the band, and the princesses are ready. I've got a lot of phone calls to make today. What are you guys doing next?"

"I think we are going to catch a movie or something. You want to go?"

"Probably not. I don't have the time. You guys go and have fun. I need to have the place to myself to make those calls anyway."

"Okay." Sam says as we walk into the living room area.

"Hey, Baby!" Ben says as he kisses me.

"Hey! Did you like Epcot?" I ask.

"Yeah, but I wish you would have come with us. It did give me a chance to buy something for you though," he said with a sly smile.

"Oh, yeah. What is it?"

"Oh, nothing," he said with a smile. He is being too suspicious this week. What is he up to?

"Are you going to the movie?"

"Nope, I need to make some calls this afternoon. I need to fill Marge in on what to do. I need to let her know which calls to forward to my cell. It's going to be a hectic week without me there."

"Oh yeah, they are starting construction on the building this week."

"Yeah, it really wasn't the best week for me to take off, but it will work out. I wanted come with you."

"You are so sweet!" I kiss him and I look over at Lynsey and Sam on the couch making out. That is really getting annoying. Ben and I don't make out in front of them. "Hey! You two! Cut it out!" I yell before I realize that I said it out loud. They both look at me with surprise and I quickly come up with something to say. "Uh, I was just kidding. Continue."

"We are going to see a movie; do you guys want to come?" Lynsey asks in her more than annoying sweet voice.

"We have calls to make today, but you guys should go and have a good time," I say.

"Well, see you guys at dinner. They are having some kind of Luau tonight. Do you want to go?" Sam asks.

"Sure. Sounds festive!" I say. With that, they left the suite. Ben and I alone in a hotel room. This can't be good.

"Hey, Baby, you want to sit for a while on the couch before we start working?" Ben asks with that sly smile of his.

"Uh, I don't know. We are in a hotel room by ourselves. I don't know what kind of temptation will enter this room if we do that."

"I just want to sit with you for a while. I haven't seen you all day."

"Okay, but don't get any ideas," I say as we plop on the couch. He kisses my cheek and then my lips. What is he up to? I know we haven't been together very long, but that kiss definitely had a commitment feeling attached. I don't want to commit. Committing means rings, weddings, and moving. Okay, I don't think so. I'm too young to make wedding plans. Well, my own plans anyway. I mean, if he's the one, that's great, but I am not getting married right now. The day that Paris Hilton gets married, then maybe I'll be ready, but not until then.

All of these thoughts fly through my mind as the make out session begins. I knew this would be a bad idea. His hand was rubbing my back when I pulled away. "I told you temptation would come in." I stand and give him my famous pout.

"Hey, I just wanted to kiss and nothing more. Are you accusing me, Ms. London, of trying to seduce you?" he asks as he kisses my neck.

"Yes, I am." I kiss him and I take my phone to the kitchen table. I have too much to do! I call and check on the cake. The man on the phone confirmed that a glitter (that still amazes me) castle cake would be at Cinderella's castle on Friday. Well, that's a good thing because a birthday party must have a cake. I learned my lesson there.

I called to confirm High School Musical and Miley Cyrus. They are ready and excited. They will perform three songs each. Their manager said that they are so excited to perform at Storm's birthday. Well, that's good because they are performing anyway. The Finn's paid big bucks for them to be there. Who cares if they are excited? The manager probably made that up.

I sent the gift bags over to Cinderella's castle. We still have our reservations by pure luck. I have to remember to give that Mark guy a tip. I think I need to call the Finn's and update them. I dial their number.

"Hello," that must be Mr. Finn.

"Hello, I'm Lora Kate London, your party planner. I just wanted to go over all of the details before the party on Friday," I say.

"Great! Let's hear it!" Mr. Finn said.

"You have reservations at Cinderella's Royal Table, the cake is ordered, the gift bags have already been sent to the castle, and the performers have been confirmed. I hope I didn't leave anything out," I say.

"That sounds great! I knew my man Ben wouldn't let us down. Who is going to perform?" he asks.

"Well, I'm quite proud of who I chose for her party. I know that all of the kids love them, so I arranged for the cast of High School Musical and Miley Cyrus to perform three of their hit songs," I say with confidence. I'm still shocked about how great I am.

"Wow, Storm and her schoolmates (schoolmates? Who says that?) are going to love it. How are you enjoying Florida? Pretty hot, huh?" he asks.

"Yes it is very hot, but we are enjoying it."

"I hope that you're hotel is accommodating. Where are staying?"

"We are at The Animal Kingdom Lodge. It's really nice. Well, I hope Storm enjoys her birthday. I know that I had fun planning it," I say in my most convincing tone.

"Me too. Well, Ms. London, I guess we will see you on Friday."

"Yes, you will," I say as I hang up the phone. I didn't realize that I had been on the phone for three hours. I'm glad that I have some great phone skills because party planning is using a lot of those skills.

Sam and Lynsey walk in holding hands and giggling. "What is so funny?" I ask.

"We watched Madagascar 2. It was better than the first," Lynsey piped in.

"Like Monty Python funny?" I ask.

"Well, not that funny, but it was good," Sam says in a British accent.

"I am Arthur, King of the Britains," I recite from The Holy Grail as I stand.

"King of the who?" Sam recites back to me. We spend the next 30 minutes reciting lines from Monty Python and The Holy Grail, laughing the entire time.

"What is that from?" Lynsey finally asks out of annoyance.

"The Holy Grail," I say with shock that she didn't know where our lines were from. "You haven't seen it?"

"No, is it new?" she asks.

"Like Moses," I say.

"We have to find it. L.K., go find one," Sam says.

"I'm on it!"

I called a cab and rode to the nearest Barnes and Nobles. I decided to load up on videos. I have a feeling we will be up all night watching movies. Sam and I watch everything including the good, bad, and in between. I grabbed Monty Python and the Holy Grail, Napoleon Dynamite, The Notebook, and Hairspray. We are going to be busy. I also stop at a local dress shop and pick up something to wear tonight. I will be noticed without looking slutty.

I make it back to the hotel room and begin getting ready for the Luau. I take my shower and curl my hair. I put it up in a twist and do the make-up thing. I run into the living room and grab my dress. Sam walks in wearing Hawaiian shorts and no shirt. I've never realized how muscular Sam is. I whistle at him.

"Hey! Cut that out! Is that what you are wearing?" he asks.

I am wearing a robe. "No, I bought a new dress to wear. I want to fit in." With that, I went back to the bedroom and saw that Lynsey was only wearing shorts and tank top.

"Do I look okay?" she asks.

"Definitely. You look so comfortable. Are you all ready for the party?"

"Yep. I'm going to go in the living room so you can get ready."

"Thanks."

I put on my dress. It has a glittery, hot pink, tank top and a shiny grass skirt, but you can't see my underwear. I have never understood why women insist on showing their underwear in public. That is like my nightmare. I always dream that people can see my underwear and are laughing at me. Anyway, the skirt has these white spandex shorts underneath. I look in the mirror. "You are hot stuff, Ms. London," I say as I put on my hot pink heels and I add a Hawaiian flower in my hair. I put my Tiffany's necklace around my neck and walk into the living room.

Sam and Ben were matching in their bare chests and Hawaiian shorts. "Wow!" They said at the same time.

"Okay, Double Mint twins, let's go," I said. Finally, I'm noticed. I am very pleased with the reaction. It's about time they showed me a little love. I was getting a little tired of being put in last place. Ben comes up behind me and kisses my neck. "Hey, you want to skip the party?" he asks.

"No, I want to go. I didn't get dressed up to stay at home." I say as we lock the suite door.

We all walked to the party together. I turned to look at Sam and Lynsey. She was giving me that evil look again. What did I do? You can look hot and I can't. Whatever, so I smile at her and she gives me a half smile. Sam, however, is giving me a blank stare. "What?" I ask him.

"Uh, nothing. You look nice tonight," he said. Lynsey slaps him and they begin whispering. Geez, Lynsey. Grow up.

"You do look hot, Babe," Ben says as he tightens his arm around my waist. (Lex and Superman all over again)

I have this feeling that something bad is going to happen. I just know it. At least the party looks awesome. We all find a seat under a straw umbrella and a girl came to our table and told us to help ourselves at the buffet. I love buffets! It's when you can get some of your money back.

After eating, the D.J. put on some Frank Sinatra. "You want to dance?" I ask Ben.

"Nah, I need to make a couple of calls. I'll be back." And he's gone again. Who are these people that he calls all day? It's Sunday. No businesses are open. Who knows?

"Hey, Loser, you want to dance? Lynsey had to go call her parents," Sam said.

"Sure. Ben is making calls too. Busy that one." We walk to the dance floor. I like dancing with Sam. I don't feel like I need to please him or even dance right. I'm just dancing. The song makes me feel sad though. I feel like Ben and I are not connecting right. I mean, he is great, but I feel like he wants something. I don't know what, but he isn't telling me. Oh, well, maybe I'm just crazy. Maybe I'm just stressing about the party. Sam interrupts my thoughts.

"Hey! You okay?" he asks as he twirls a finger around one of my curls.

"Yeah, just stressed about the party, I guess."

"Everything will be great! Lynsey looks up to you. She wants to be a party planner too. I really need to say that I'm sorry. I thought that this job would be a bust, but you are really good at it."

"Thanks. I really like it too. You know, I miss this."

"What? Dancing?"

"No, us. Our friendship. Since we are in relationships, we don't just hang out anymore."

"We hang out, our friendship has just changed. That's all."

"It just feels different. I feel like I can't be myself around you if Lynsey is around."

"I feel the same about you and Ben."

"But Lynsey gives me looks."

"Ben gives me looks too."

"Maybe we should tell them that we are old friends. They shouldn't feel weird around us. Maybe a vacation together wasn't a good idea yet."

"Maybe."

When the song was over, we sat down and waited on Lynsey and Ben. Lynsey finally sat down at the table. Her face is so red. What did she do, run back to the table? "Lynsey, are you okay? You look flushed," I ask.

"Oh, yeah. I'm fine. Must be a sunburn or something," she said. That's odd...a sunburn on a perfectly tan girl who lived here for a long time?

About five minutes later, Ben walked to the table. His hair looks funny and he is wearing a shirt. He wasn't wearing a shirt. "Hey! Where'd you get the shirt?" I ask him.

"Oh, I went back to the room and got it. I felt a little chilly," he said. I'm burning up! He must be cold natured or something. He kissed my cheek and sat down. There is some kind of bad mojo stirring here.

"Ladies and Gents, please have a seat and welcome our guest entertainment, Justin Timberlake!" the announcer yelled.

We danced while Justin brought sexy back. And after the show, Ben got Justin to autograph my tank top. So now, my $300 top has Justin Timberlake printed on the stomach. Awesome!

We walked back to the suite and changed into our pajamas. I announced that we are going to have a movie marathon and no one is allowed to sleep.

"Uh, Baby, I'm tired. I don't know if I can stay up," Ben says.

"Nope! No sleeping! No Napping! Just watching a mix of the greatest movies ever," I say as I pop in Monty Python and the Holy Grail. Sam cuddles with Lynsey on the couch and Ben falls into the recliner. He pats his lap. I crawl into his lap and look over at Sam and Lynsey. I hope they don't make out during the movie. I push play and the movie begins.

Ben kisses my neck, and then my ear, and then my cheeks. I look at him. He gives me a passionate kiss. Okay, I wasn't ready for that. "Stop," I whisper. "Watch," I say in a sweet voice.

I love this movie! I didn't realize how into it I was until I looked over at Ben. He was asleep! How can you fall asleep during The Holy Grail? It's a classic! I look over at Lynsey and Sam. Lynsey is asleep! What losers! "Sam, your girlfriend and my boyfriend fell asleep in the middle of Monty Python."

"I know. It's like they don't know what funny is. I guess we will just have to finish the marathon alone, huh?"

"Yeah. Just like old times."

"Just like old times."

Chapter 14

When I woke up, I was lying on Sam's arm. Oh, crap! I fell asleep. I glance around and Lynsey and Ben are not here. I guess they went to bed last night. I look over at Sam. He is snoring and smashed against the couch. "Sam," I whisper.

"What?" he mumbles.

"It's morning. We fell asleep to Napoleon. We never fall asleep during Napoleon Dynamite."

"I was tired. We've seen it a hundred times anyway."

"I know, but its Napoleon and Pedro. Ben and Lynsey must have gone to bed because they aren't here."

"What?" He pulled himself up and looked around. "Where did they go?"

"Uh, probably to bed. That's what I just said. Listen up, Grandpa!"

"Shut up, Loser!"

"You shut up," I say as I hop up. "I think I'm going to go for a run," I say as I put on my shoes.

"You, running. Yeah, right."

"Shut up! I run sometimes."

"Yeah, when something's chasing you" he said as he put on his shoes and looked at me with a smile.

"Well, I'll just have to pretend."

"Or not." He got up and chased me out the front door. Run, Forrest, Run! I ran as fast as I could, but I started to get a cramp in my side. Man, I'm out of shape! I need to run more. I need a doughnut. I need coffee. We ran all the way to the swimming pool. He grabbed me and threw me into the pool.

"You jerk! I'm wearing all of my clothes and this shirt was fifty bucks!"

"So, it was funny. At least you didn't trip, klutz." He was standing near the edge of the pool laughing at me. I swam over and pulled him in too.

"I will be revenged!" I yell as I dunk his head under the cool, blue water.

"Hey! You two, Out of the pool! It's not open!" A man yelled.

"Oh, sorry. We accidentally fell in," we yell as we scramble out of the pool. "I can't believe you threw me into the pool. What are you, ten?"

"Yeah. Hey, you pulled me in."

"I was getting revenge. I had purpose."

"So did I."

"I need coffee and doughnuts."

"We just got through running. You can't eat like that after you exercise."

"Why not? I was going to eat it anyway, but now I have burned enough calories that it evens it out."

"That makes no sense."

"I think it does."

I open the door to the suite and see Lynsey sitting at the table in a towel and Ben is massaging her shoulders. Okay, I know I'm not the brightest crayon in the box, but this is not good. What is going on? I look at Sam. He was feeling the same way.

"Hey guys! What's up? Where have you been and why are you guys all wet?" Lynsey says like nothing weird is going on.

"Uh, we went running this morning and fell into the pool. What are you guys doing?" I ask.

"Ben was massaging my shoulder. I think sleeping on the couch messed it up. It really hurts. Sam, will you take over?" she asks in a whiny voice.

Huh! Well, he'd better. She could have put on some clothes. How rude. Sam walks over to Lynsey. I think he is stunned too. The picture just didn't look good. Ben scoops me up and kisses me.

"Hey, Baby! How was your run?" Ben asks.

"Fine. How was Lynsey?" I ask as he puts a towel around me.

"What do you mean? She asked me to rub her shoulders. Was I supposed to be rude and say no?"

"Yes."

"What about you and Sam? How was your swim?"

"It was an accident. I went running this morning for exercise. Not to play games."

"Okay. I'm sorry. Are we okay?"

"I guess. How about a kiss?" He kisses me and throws me on the bed. We were kissing when I felt his hand on my stomach.

"Okay. That's enough, Romeo. I'm going to shower. I kiss him on the cheek and went into the living room.

Sam and Lynsey are kissing. I notice that her towel fell a little and her entire top half is completely exposed. Crap! I pull her towel up and shove her into the bedroom. "Okay. You cannot wear your towel around the suite. It's not appropriate," I say as I pull my wet clothes off and pull a robe around me.

"But you can come in soaking wet with my boyfriend?"

"Lynsey, we are friends. We have been friends. We went running. That's it. It's not like you and Sam are completely committed in a deep relationship. I mean, what were you doing with Ben? Sam does not rub my shoulders. He just doesn't. I really don't want to fight about this. I just didn't want the world seeing your chest, okay?"

"Fine. I don't want to fight either. Maybe this wasn't the best time for all of us to vacation together."

"I'm beginning to feel the same way." I've said it and thought it a hundred times before.

I took a shower and tried to wash the whole morning off of me. I know I spent at least an hour in there. I got dressed in my jeans with all of the holes (I have no idea why they are so popular and so expensive now. It makes no sense to me, but they are comfortable and I love them) and a purple tank top. I don't care what I look like today. I put my hair into a ponytail and walked into the living room. Ben was in jeans and a Polo.

"Hey, Baby!" I say as I flop onto his lap.

"You look cute."

"Thanks. What's our plan today?"

"I thought we might go shopping today. I thought that you might like having a little shopping spree on my credit card. What do you say?"

"What do I say? Heck, Yeah! I'm going on a shopping spree. I'm so excited just like Julia Roberts in Pretty Woman. Well, kind of. Are Sam and Lynsey going too?"

"Umm, how about just you and me today, Babe?"

"I say, yes." I told Sam and Lynsey where we were going and then we left.

We took a Limo into town. I feel like a movie star. You know, I've been told that I look a lot like Jessica Simpson, which is a total lie. Maybe I'll buy a dog and some cowboy boots and start a singing career. Or not. I can't sing and I look terrible in short shorts.

"L.K., what are you thinking about?" Ben asks.

"Shorts and dogs."

"Is that what you want?"

"No. I don't want either. I was just thinking."

"I need more coffee if I'm going to keep up with you today."

"Me too. Let's stop somewhere. Somewhere cozy."

"How about Starbucks?"

"No way. That is not cozy. That is a busy, creepy place. Sorry. No can do."

"Why? I like it."

"How about over there?" I point at a little coffee place on the corner.

"Okay. Driver, please pull over to the left at Mocha Joe's please," Ben says.

"Okay, Mr. Sparks. Right away," the driver says as he pulls over.

"We will be here for about thirty minutes. Thanks." Ben helps me out of the Limo and we walk into the shop. The aroma of coffee overwhelms me. I love coffee. All of the flavors. I look at the menu and try to decide what to get (Carmel Macchiato, um, too sweet), (Mocha, no), (Mint? Yuck!). I decide to get the biggest regular cup of coffee they have and I go find a corner booth.

Ben and I sip our coffee in silence. He reads the Wall Street Journal and I read US Weekly. What a match! I am so content right now. I'm having one those Zen feelings like one of those Yoga instructors. All happy and at peace.

"Ladies and Gentlemen, welcome a newcomer to the stage," a lady says into a microphone. Well, so much for Zen. "Welcome this lovely poet, Mr. James Madden." What? James Madden. Crap! I look up from US Weekly and there he is, tall and annoying, James Madden. I look over at Ben. He is boiling inside. I can tell. James must have followed us out here to spy on the party. I can't believe this! What is he doing up there?

"Out of the window, I peer at night. Looking at my success as man," he says. Whatever! He is just jealous of Ben. I can't believe he is here. I've got to do something. I look around and everyone is enthralled with James' performance.

"What is he doing?" I whisper to Ben.

"Trying to ruin me. Let's go," he says as he stands up.

"Okay." I get up and decide to walk over to James. I take the pitcher of water sitting on the counter and I throw it on him. Every icy drop. I feel liberated and I can't get fired from this coffee shop. I turn on my heel and walk out with my head up, but have to turn around before I open the door. "That's what you get for spying, you....you spy!" What an idiot. Can I not think of any other words? Good grief.

"What did you just do?" Ben asks as we get into the Limo.

"I made my revenge. Let's say he got the picture that we know what he's up to."

"I'm not even going to ask you to explain."

"Good. Let's go shopping."

The driver pulls into the mall and parks in front of the mall entrance. I feel so important. Everyone is staring at us. I bet they are wondering what celebrity is coming to shop. Maybe I should leave my sunglasses on. I grab my Louis Vuitton bag and step out of the Limo. Ben and I walk into the mall with all eyes on me. My cell phone starts to ring. Ah, Man! I flip it open, "Hello."

"L.K., where are you?" my mother asks.

"Orlando, why?"

"Your father and I came home to find Gerta and her husband. Naked! On our kitchen table! You were supposed to watch the house, Honey."

"Mom, you knew I was leaving. I saw Gerta naked too."

"Well, what did you do about it?"

"Nothing. I got my luggage and got the heck out. What was I supposed to do?"

"You supposed to tell Gerta that she cannot do that."

"I'm not her boss. You are."

"Oh, L.K. I loved Gerta. She cooked the best dinners."

"Did you fire her?"

"Well, I had to. She was having sex on my kitchen table, Lora Kate. I can't have her working for me if she is going to have sex in my home. I'm going to have to buy a new table."

"Well, you better buy a new living room suit too. They probably had sex all over the house."

"Oh, gross, L.K. Now I have to buy everything new."

"I'm sure that makes you so sad, Mom. Is there anything else?"

"No, but I did buy you lots of things from Rome."

"That's great, Mom, but I have to go. I'm shopping."

"Bye, Honey." With that, I hung up and pulled Ben into Hollister.

I love malls. Everything is so fast paced. The people, the shops, the music. I can't get enough of it. We bought a smoothie and sat down on a bench. "What is your favorite thing about shopping?" I ask Ben.

"Um, I guess I enjoy knowing that I can spend as much as I want."

"I guess, but I love the free samples and the candy store. We have to go there before we leave."

"Whatever you want, Babe."

I pulled Ben into every store. He had to call his driver to come pick up some of the bags before we could move on. I love shopping. It's a stress reliever. I think I bought something in every store. He said I could have whatever I wanted and I just happen to want everything. I found the perfect gift for Sam and candy too, of course. I bought Lynsey some jeans and T-shirt that will cover her pre K-Fed Britney Spears body.

I also bought Ben some pajamas that have The Animal from the Muppets on them. I know that he is paying for everything, but I had to get him something. Poor guy. He is sitting on a bench somewhere wondering when I'll be finished. I have one store left and I cannot leave the mall without making an appearance.

I walk into Barnes and Nobles and sigh. The powerful smell overwhelms me. I smell a sale. A big sale. I search for the bargain tables and hit the jackpot. I walk out of the store with six bags full of books.

I find Ben sitting near the escalator. "Poor, Baby, are you bored?" I ask him.

"A little. I've been watching this kid going up and down on the escalator. Not very interesting."

"That kid is back on the escalator!" I recite.

"What?"

"Do you ever watch movies?"

"Not a lot."

"Apparently. That is from Mallrats. Hey, what's in the bag?" I notice he shopped a little too.

"Surprise."

"I like surprises. You ready?"

"About 4 hours ago."

"Sorry." We get into the Limo. "I'm hungry. Can we go through a drive-thru in the Limo?"

"I guess. What for?"

"How cool would it be to go through a McDonald's drive-thru in a Limo?"

"Cool, I guess. Driver, Ms. London would like to go through the McDonald's drive-thru to order lunch." That sounds so cool.

"Yes, Mr. Sparks," he says.

"What's the driver's name?"

"I don't know."

"Well, ask him."

"You ask him."

I sigh, "Fine. Hey, Mr. Limo driver, what's your name?"

"Tyler, ma'am."

"Thanks, Tyler."

We went through McDonald's and ordered lunch. I ate my Big Mac on the way back to the suite. I am eating a Big Mac in a Limo! I'm so fancy! We pull into the suite and Ben stops me before I go in. He hands me the bag. "What is it?"

"Open it."

I pull the tissue out of the bag and there, lying in the bottom of this pink bag, is that same slutty, red dress that I threw in the back of my closet! How do I react? Should I smile? Should I run? What do I do? I look up at him and smile.

"I made sure that I got the right size this time."

"Thanks, Baby! It's...nice." Oh, my gosh! It is the ugliest dress ever! I cannot wear this.

"You can wear it to dinner tonight."

What! I can't wear this to dinner. What will people think? I know exactly what people will think. They are going wonder why I'm not on my corner. "Great! Thanks." I hug him as I roll my eyes.

This is going to be an interesting night when my boob flops out on the fine, white linen. Maybe I will suggest we go to Hooters. At least I would fit in.

We walk into the suite while the driver brings in all of my bags. "Geez, L.K., did you buy the entire mall?" Sam asks.

"No, just half of it. I bought you and Lynsey some stuff."

"Oh, yeah. Show us!"

"Settle down. I'll show you." I pull out the clothes for Lynsey.

"Thanks, L.K. I love them! They are so cute! I'm so glad that we are the same size and have the same taste."

"Now me!" Sam begs.

"Okay, Rover, settle down, you'll get your treat." I pull out a brand new Peanuts shirt just like the one that he has, but it's new and doesn't contain holes in the pits.

"Oh, my gosh! You found it! You are the greatest!" He hugs me so tight that I couldn't breath.

"Okay, Sam, you can let go now." He let me go and I hand him the candy I bought for him.

"Where did you find these?"

"I was at the mall all day. Where do you think I found them, Dummy? I knew you loved Razzles, so I got some."

"Thank you. Thank you very much." Sam says in his best Elvis voice.

I can't believe that this day is almost over. It won't be long until I have to supervise that party. I really hope everything goes okay. I still can't shake the feeling of upcoming drama. We have already had a bad run in with James. Now what?

"Hey, you guys want to eat dinner somewhere nice?" Ben asks.

"Like Hooters?" I ask.

"What? That's not nice, that's cheap," he says.

Just like my dress.

I spent the next hour looking at myself in the mirror and contemplating all the ways that I could be humiliated wearing this dress. I tried covering it with sweaters, scarves, even robes. Nothing worked. Nothing on this Earth could cover this dress.

"L.K., what are you doing?" Lynsey asks.

"Trying to cover this dress."

"It's not that bad. It's really pretty on you."

"It's not my taste. It's Show Girls. It's the same one he bought me before we came here. You didn't like it then."

"Well, I kind of did, but I didn't want to disagree with you."

"Well, I hate it. It's just not me, but he is determined that I wear this dress. I'm just glad that no one I know will see me. I guess I should just suck it up and wear it."

"I guess so."

I put on my red heels to match my "dress" and went to the living room to sulk. I wish I could fake sick and stay in. I would love to put on my pajamas and just hang out. I want to order a pizza and watch The Notebook. I don't want to wear the dress. I feel like I did when I was four when Mom made me wear a sailor outfit to preschool. Why do parents dress their children in clothes that they hate? Why do boyfriends buy clothes for their girlfriends? I'll never know the answer to these two questions.

"Hey, sexy!" Sam shouts.

"Shut up, Loser! You know I hate this." I whisper.

"The night will be over soon and you can come back and wear pajamas."

"You're right. I'll wear the dress without complaining."

Ben walks in and I stand and spin around. I want him to fully see that I'm wearing this dress and to burn the image into his brain because I'm not wearing it again. "What do you think?" I ask him.

"Very sexy, Babe," he says.

"Good, let's go." Lynsey and Sam followed behind us to the Limo.

Tyler drove us to a very nice restaurant. I can't even pronounce the name. That scares me. I can never find anything to order when I can't understand the language. The hostess walks us to our table. We all sit and the she says, "Thank you, Mr. Sparks. It's so nice to see you again." That's weird, has he been here before?

"Thank you, Jennifer. It's nice to be back here again," Ben says. Okay, I have to know what is going on here.

After she walks away, I ask, "Who was that?"

"Oh, that's Jennifer. She used to work for me in New York. We used to date. She had to move with her family, so we broke it off." Crap! Did I want to know that? Was she special to him? And why did he say it was nice to be back? Had he visited her? Oh, man. There is still so much to learn about him.

"Oh. Um…" Before I could finish, the waiter came. Thank you! The waiter gave us menus and left. I glance at it for like two seconds. I can't read French, but I try to find something that sounds like chicken. You can't lose with chicken. Sam looks confused too. I think I'll order after him so I won't sound like an idiot.

"What does everyone want?" Ben asks.

"I just want some chicken?" I ask.

"Me too," Sam says.

"Do you want me to order for you?" Ben asks.

"Please," Sam and I say.

Lynsey said, "I can order my own."

"Good for you," I say. I hate when people can do things that I can't. I want to know another language. I wonder if Pig Latin is considered as a foreign language. I can speak that.

After the waiter brings our food, we eat in silence. In my life, I have discovered that anything smothered in a cheese sauce is good. The more I get to know Ben and Lynsey, the more I'm surprised. I wonder what's up with the Jennifer girl. Do I want to know? Probably not.

I was completely lost in thought when I felt icy cold water run down my back! I turn around and James is standing there with a huge smile on his face. "Okay, Skinny, you and me, outside!" I yell as I stand from my chair. He follows me outside in front of the restaurant.

"Sorry, but I had to get you back," he says.

"You could have done it somewhere else. I'm freezing now in this dress and this is a very nice place," I say as I point to the restaurant.

"Here, take my coat." He puts his coat around me and I secretly thank God for this. I needed something to cover my bare body.

"Thanks."

"I just wanted you to know that I didn't come here to spy. I came here with my fiancé. I didn't even know that you were here. Now that I do, I should spy. I want to see this party of yours. You are already getting street cred back home. Maybe I can make you a better offer."

"I doubt it. I'm head planner. If I were any higher, I would be Ben."

"All of his girls are head planners."

"What does that mean?"

"I stay on top of things. One of his girls was head planner for a long time, but she moved or something. I don't remember."

"Wait a minute! Was her name, Jennifer?"

"I'm not sure. Why?"

"Nothing. I was just wondering. Okay, maybe things are different with me."

"For your sake, I hope you're right. You've got some real talent. It's raw talent and I like it. Well, sorry about the water. It was pretty funny. You have to admit it."

"I guess. Bye, James."

"Bye, L.K." He takes off and I go back into the restaurant.

I totally forgot that I was wearing his jacket. Oh, well. I sit back down and everyone is looking at me. "What?" I ask.

"What happened?" Sam asks.

"Well, I beat him up and took his jacket," I say.

"What really happened?" Ben asks with anger in his eyes.

"Well, he apologized for the water and explained that he wasn't spying on us. He and his fiancé are just here by coincidence."

"Oh, sure. He is such a liar. Did he offer you a job and why are you wearing his jacket?" Ben asks.

"I was freezing and he did spill the water on me so he offered his coat. He was apologizing. He did offer me a job."

"Are you serious?"

"Yes, but I turned him down politely."

"Oh. Well, is everyone ready to go?" Ben asks.

"Yes," we all agreed.

The ride home was quiet. Lynsey was asleep on Sam's arm and Ben was looking out the window. "What's up?" I ask him.

"Nothing. I'm just thinking."

"Oh, about what?"

"You."

"Me?"

"Yeah. I was thinking that you and I could have had a special night together tonight."

"It was special."

"Well, with Jennifer and James. I don't know how special it was."

"What's up with this Jennifer?"

"She and I were really close and it ended. I don't know how, but it did. I really did care about her, but it was so long ago it seems. My relationship with you feels like it did with her. Not in a creepy way, but in a good way. I really like you."

"Well, I'm glad, but James did tell me some things about you and your girls."

"Like what kind of things?"

"He said that all of your girls have been head planners. Is that true?"

"Of course not. He just wants you to quit and come work for him. You don't realize what kind of talent you have. No one in all my years as a man in the party business see someone with no experience plan such elite parties. You are good, Ms. Lora Kate London and don't let Jennifer bother you. That is in the past."

"Oh. Well, how can we make this night better?"

"Sleep."

"Okay."

We all walked into the suite together and all went to our beds. This trip just keeps getting more interesting. Even though tonight was pretty weird for me and Ben, I still keep thinking of Sam and Lynsey. I don't know if Lynsey is Sam's type. I don't know what girl is Sam's type. He needs someone who will understand him, let him be himself, and someone who makes him laugh. He needs someone he can trust. With that thought, I fell asleep.

Chapter 15

I woke up to the sound of a cell ringing. Who in the world is calling this early? I listen and hear Lynsey stir and say hello. "What? Oh yeah, he's definitely giving me the internship. There's no way he is going to turn me down now. Oh, yeah, he has a girlfriend. She's my roommate. I know! It's crazy! Shut up! I've gotta go. Bye, Steph." With that, she hung up and went back to sleep. Who was that and what did she mean? I turn over and look at her. She is so content. I don't know why she rubs me the wrong way. If she didn't annoy me so much, I would love her.

I decide to forget it and go back to sleep. There's too much drama in Orlando. I'm ready to go back to NYC! It wasn't long until

Sam was jumping on my bed screaming, "Get up, Loser! We're going to Disney World!"

"Go away, Sam! Some of us want to sleep!"

"Everyone is ready to go. Get up!"

"Ugh!" I crawled out of bed and put a robe over my neon green nightie. "You are like ten today."

"We are going to the happiest place on earth. I have a right to act like a kid."

"Okay, Sammy. Now, leave me alone so I can get dressed."

"We are going to ride every ride and eat at every restaurant just like the time we went to Knott's Berry Farm. Do you remember that? I gained like ten pounds on that trip."

"It was a celebration for actually graduating from college with a degree and everything. We had some fun times together, huh?"

"We still do. Now, get ready," he says as he shuts my door.

I finally have the room to myself. I take a hot shower and get dressed in a pink tank top and jean shorts. I lace up my tennis shoes and walk into the living room where everyone is standing at the door ready to go. "Okay, I'm ready," I say as I grab a cup of coffee.

"It's about time, turtle," Sam laughs as he pokes me in the sides.

"Lynsey, you are going to have to put a leash on him today. He is acting like a five year old," I say smiling. I am determined to be in a good mood today.

"I know, right? He has been giggling all over the suite this morning," she says.

"So, where's the Limo?" I ask Ben.

Ben says with a smirk, "I had a different idea for transportation today."

A man in a horse and buggy pulls up to the hotel. "Surprise!" Ben says. "A carriage for my lady!"

"Awesome!" I hop in and make myself comfortable. My boyfriend is so cool. "I have the best boyfriend in the whole world."

"Do you also have the prettiest pony in all the land?" Sam asks.

I give him a look and say, "Don't you ruin this. This is my special present and I'm going to enjoy it."

We took the buggy all the way to the park. Sam helped Lynsey out, but when Ben stepped out to help me, my foot got caught on the step and of course, I fall. Okay, this time it's not so funny. My foot hurts really badly and everyone is laughing which is normal. Okay, I can't get up! I didn't realize that I had tears running down my face.

"Baby, are you okay?" Ben said as he tried to help me up.

"Stop! I can't move and no, I'm not okay. I think something is broke!"

"Do you think we need an ambulance?"

"What? No, I don't want to go to the hospital on vacation."

"Well, we might have to. I don't think we have a choice here. Driver, dial 911! We need some help here!"

My foot really hurts. This totally sucks. I have a party to go to on Friday. I can't run around a kid's birthday party in a cast. I hope that it's not broken. I didn't even get to see Mickey Mouse. Well, this just stinks.

"Okay, I'm riding in the ambulance," Sam says.

Ben raises his voice, "No, I think I should ride in the ambulance. I am her boyfriend."

"Okay, I think both of you morons should shut up!" I yell at them. "Flip a coin or something!"

"Fine! Lynsey, flip a coin. I call heads," Ben says.

"I was kidding! I don't want you flipping any coins." No one seems to hear me. "Hello, I'm the one in pain here." Lynsey flips the quarter and it lands on tails.

"Hah! I get to ride in the ambulance. Cool," Sam says.

"I'm so glad that you two are delighting in my pain. I say you both can ride in the ambulance and I'll stay here on the ground!" I yell back. I am in such a bad mood now. No Mickey Mouse. No Haunted Mansion. And no Space Mountain. This really sucks!

"You're right. You can choose who rides with you," Sam says.

"Oh, right! Make me choose. That's fair!" I scream.

Finally, the ambulance arrives. They pick me up and put me on the stretcher. I have to admit it is pretty cool. Inside the ambulance, the EMT asks who was riding with me. "You choose. I'm tired of thinking about it," I say.

"Are any of them family?" he asks.

"No, but I guess I would call Sam family. I have known him the longest, but Ben is my boyfriend and Lynsey is my roommate. What do you think?"

"I would say Sam, I guess. I have never had to choose someone to take. Usually, someone just hops in." He sticks his head out and says, "Sam, you get in. Apparently, I got the option to choose someone to ride in the ambulance."

Sam hops in, sits beside me, and takes my hand. That's strange because we have never held hands like this. It's not like I'm dying. It does feel nice though. "So, what are Ben and Lynsey going to do?" I ask.

"Oh, man! I forgot to tell them to follow us."

"Well, it's no big deal. They should just go into the park. It's not like I have an illness or something. It's not Steel Magnolias. I'll be fine."

"I guess. I think they are behind us in a cab. I didn't think that Ben would ride in a cab with all the Limos and Carriages."

"Oh, come on. You know that you have had a good time." The EMT was checking my vitals and putting a pillow behind my head. This is kind of nice except Sam keeps fiddling with everything. The EMT looked at Sam with a look that said, "Stop touching!"

Sam looks at me with uneasy eyes and says, "I guess I've had a good time."

"You guess?"

"Yeah. I don't know if Lynsey is really into me. I think she keeps avoiding me. We start kissing and she pulls away. She has been talking on the phone a lot too. When I ask who she's talking to, she tells me just a friend. This trip has been too weird. I'm ready to go home, to be honest."

"Me too."

When we finally got the hospital, we had to wait forever in the waiting room. The EMT put me into one of those wheel chairs that put your legs up. It was very uncomfortable. Lynsey and Ben walked into the hospital and found us sitting in a corner waiting. How boring. They never have good magazines in the waiting rooms.

"Hey, how do you feel?" Lynsey asks.

I say, "I'm in pain, but I guess I'm okay."

Ben kisses my cheek and holds my hand. "How was the ride?" he asks.

"Boring. Sam got in trouble with the EMT guy. So that was pretty entertaining."

"I wish I could have been with you."

"It was no big deal."

"Ms. London?" the nurse asks.

"Over here!" I yell. Finally, I've been waiting forever.

The nurse rolled me into X-ray and took a lot of pictures of my foot. Now I'm just waiting in a little room with pictures of organs on the wall. Why in the world do doctors think we want to look at organs and bones while we wait in a hospital room? They should fill them with comforting pictures like puppies and flowers. I hate hospitals. They smell weird and you have to sit on the paper bed and wait. It's torture.

The doctor walks in and smiles. I've got the cute doctor today. I know, I'm with Ben, but this guy is a doctor! "Hello. I'm Dr. Gipson, but you can call me Shad. How are you today, Ms. London?" he asks in a sexy voice.

"Perfect, Shad" I said. He is so gorgeous.

He looks at me smiling. "How about the foot?" he asks.

"Well, not exactly perfect. Is it broken?"

"I'm afraid so. I'm going to fit you for a cast and some crutches. You should be able to go home in a few hours."

"Well, I'm actually on vacation. My home is New York."

"I'm so sorry. Breaking your foot on vacation was not exactly on your agenda. I hope that you'll be able to enjoy the rest of your vacation."

"Yeah. I'm actually working right now too. I'm a party planner."

"Oh, yeah. What kind of parties?"

"Anything. Why? Do you have an event that needs a planner?"

"Not right now, but I'll take your number for when I need you."

Oh my gosh! He wants my number. I know I'm totally with Ben, but he is super sexy and he won't call me anyway. I jot down my number on the paper bed and rip the piece off. "Here you go," I say as I hand him my number.

"Well, I was thinking more along the lines of a business card, but this will do."

"Oh, sorry. I didn't bring them with me. I didn't exactly plan on advertising in the hospital."

"True. Well, Ms. London, I'll see you again after they put your cast on."

"Okay. Thanks." With that, he was gone. How sad. Dr. Shad Gipson. So sexy.

They put my cast on and gave me some crutches. Crap! This vacation is going to have to end quickly. I don't know how much more I can take. I'm cranky and I'm ready to see Mom. I want to go back to my apartment and watch Friends with Mrs. Tragger. I want to sit on my elevator bench and drink coffee. I even miss Gerta, the naked maid.

My cast is hot pink. If I'm going to be in a cast, I'm going to be in style. Dr. Gipson was the first one to sign my cast. He also wrote his phone number below his name. You know, just in case I needed him for anything. When I walk into the lobby, all my friends are gone. Where did they go? Hello! I need a ride back to the suite! I ask the receptionist if I had any messages and she hands me a slip of paper with cash attached. "L.K., take a cab back to the suite. We will meet you there. Love, Us." Great. I'm in a cast and they leave me. I'm so loving my friends today.

The suite was completely empty when I opened the door. Well, now I have to sit here alone in the dark. I am so mad. No, I am furious! I flop on the couch and throw my crutches on the floor. This totally sucks. I decide to sleep off my anger and hopefully feel better when I wake up. Only three more days.

I could feel someone looking at me. I open my eyes and glared at Ben. "What?"

"Hey, Baby, I brought ice cream." He says as I lift myself up. I hate when someone wakes me up. I'm not exactly pleasant.

"Where in the world have you been?" I ask in my Wicked Witch voice.

"Well, we went to Disney World."

"Without me? You let me sit here in my cast, my cast, while you all skipped merrily to Mickey Land. I'm appalled!" I hop to my room and slam the door. How dare them! I can't wait until Friday. I'm so ready to go home!

Someone knocks at the door. "What!"

"Can I come in?" Ben asks.

"I guess."

"Hey, I'm sorry. The nurse told us you would probably be at the hospital for hours. We thought that we would beat you back. I bought you something from every store. Sam, Lynsey, and I got every character's autograph and we took tons of pictures for you. I feel so bad."

"Well, you should. I was in pain and you guys went to the park. That was low. You bought me stuff?" My ears perk up.

"Yeah. Lots of stuff. Do you want to eat?"

"What did you get?"

"Pizza."

"Supreme?"

"Yeah."

"No Olives?"

"Sam said that was one of your favorites. You want some?"

"I guess, but I'm still mad at all of you."

We spent the rest of the night piled up in Sam's bed watching Friends and eating a "Joey Special, two pizzas." It was nice. Lynsey signed my cast and drew a little butterfly by her name. Sam covered most of the cast with his name and a picture of Charlie Brown and not a very good one by the way. Ben signed his name and wrote, "I love you." Now, I don't know what to think about that. We have never said that. I think it is too soon. Maybe it's a sympathy "I love you" and not an "I love love you." I don't think we are ready for that.

"Okay, I'm ready for bed," I say.

"Really, it's early," Lynsey said.

"Well, I've had a long day. I think I'm going to go to my room and sleep. Besides, the pills they gave me at the hospital are making me loopy."

"Do you want me to sit with you for a while?" Ben asks.

"No, I'm not dying. I just want to sleep."

"You know, I'm pretty tired too," Sam said yawning.

"Well, I'm not," Lynsey said. "Why don't you take my bed until I'm ready to sleep?"

"Uh, I guess. Is that okay?" he asks as he looks over to me.

"What do I care? I'm going to be asleep."

"Okay, then." Sam kisses Lynsey and we go to my room.

"Did that seem…?" He asks.

"Weird?"

"Yeah, weird."

"I think this whole trip has been weird."

"Me too. So, how are you really doing?"

"I'm really okay. It doesn't hurt much. Dr. Shad said that it should be fine."

"Dr. Shad?" he asks with a smile.

"Oh, yeah. He was my very sexy doctor today."

"What about Ben?"

"I like Ben. I just thought he was cute."

"You never cease to amaze me. Just when I thought you and Ben were getting too serious, you tell me about your sexy doctor. I mean Ben wrote that he loves you on your cast."

"I know. I saw that too. I'm hoping it's just sympathy. We haven't been dating that long."

"I know. It's good to know you aren't moving too fast."

I look over at him from my bed. "I'm not moving too fast. What about you and Lynsey? Every time I look at you guys, you are kissing. Well, not lately, but most of the time."

"Not so much lately. I've been doing a lot of thinking. I'd rather forget about it right now. Let's sleep. Good night."

"Night."

I was dreaming about French Fries when I suddenly woke up. What time is it? I look over and Sam is still in Lynsey's bed. The clock says, "3:33 a.m." How weird. Where is Lynsey? I figured that she would have kicked Sam out already. I pull myself up on my crutches and hop into the living room. Lynsey is walking out of Ben's room. "Hey!"

"Whoa! You scared me half to death!" she gasps.

"Sorry, I was wondering where you were." Her hair looks like crap and she is wearing shorts. When did she put on shorts?

"Oh, I fell asleep," she huffs. What is her problem? I just asked a question! I am so sick of getting the shaft on this stupid vacation.

"And just for your information, Ben was in the other bed. I did not fall asleep right next to him like you did with Sam earlier this week."

"Okay, Lynsey, I am totally sorry about that. Sam and I are such good friends. I would never try to steal him from you. He's like my brother."

"Oh, I'm not worried about you. I'm worried about him. He loves you."

"Well, sure he does. We are best friends. I love him too."

"Not like he loves you. He has got the hots for you and I can see it. You didn't come in soaking wet from the pool because you guys are friends."

"Oh, Lynsey, it's nothing and I'm not worried about you and Ben. Can't we trust each other? You are my roommate. We can't be like this. Please don't be angry with me."

"I'm not angry at you. Well, not anymore. Hey, did I tell you that Ben gave me an internship?"

"No, that's cool. How did you ask him?"

"Oh, I just waited for the right moment. I have a way of being persuasive and getting my way."

"Well, that's great, Lynsey. Maybe you can intern under me. I'd love the help. I'm going back to bed, but I am glad that Ben gave you an internship. That's really cool of him." This is unbelievable. I can't believe she is accusing Sam of being in love with me. I need to forget all about this. I insist on making this vacation the best. God, you gotta help me out here. I need all sorts of help. I need a good attitude and apparently I need some patience. I don't want to be mean to Lynsey, but she's making it hard. S.O.S!

Chapter 16

Wednesday completely flew by. We went back to Disney World even though I was on crutches. I did get to rent one of those wheelchairs though. That was cool because I didn't have to walk all day. Sam complained the entire time because he had already seen everything. I reminded him about how I got the shaft and he shut up.

Ben took me out on Thursday night alone. He asked me to wear the red dress again so that everything could be perfect. So, again, I was completely humiliated in the dress, but now it will be complete with a cast. We drove to the beach and he carried me to a blanket in the sand. He had everything set up and it was really romantic! There were candles everywhere. I started to freak out though. This has commitment written all over it.

"What's going on?" I ask.

"I wanted us to have a perfect night here in paradise."

"Oh, it kind of reminds me of the Friends episode with the one where Ross and Rachel, you know."

"Does it?"

"Yeah, kind of weird. Why did you want me to dress up if we were coming to the beach? I would have brought my suit. Well, then again, I couldn't swim because of my beautiful cast."

"I don't think you'll need it."

"I am not skinny dipping. I've watched all the scary movies. Bad things happen to people who skinny dip in the ocean at night."

He gives me a smirk. "Well, I didn't actually want to go skinny dipping."

"Well, then, what did you want to do?" Okay, I'm an idiot. I think he wants to have sex on the beach. Isn't that some sort of drink? I can't have sex on the beach in a cast. Wait a minute! I can't have sex! What in the world am I going to do? I have to call Sam. I need a rescuer! "Um, I need to use the bathroom. I'll be right back."

I hobble to the car on my crutches and call Sam. "Sam, help! I need you to come to the beach, like, now. I think Ben wants to do, you know."

"What?"

"Sam, you know! Sex!"

"Okay, I'm on my way." With that, he hung up and I creep slowly back to Ben. How am I going to stall?

"Feel better?"

"Huh? Oh, yeah, much better."

"Good." He grabs my crutches and pulls me down on the blanket. He kisses my neck. "Tonight is going to be our night, L.K."

"What exactly do you mean by our night?" I am so desperately trying to stall.

"I think it's time to move our relationship to the next level." What is that? Why is there any need for levels? It sounds like a game.

"Do you mean saying I love you?" I ask.

"Well, I don't know if we are quite there yet."

"Well, that's a relief. I thought you wanted to say I love you because of what you wrote on my cast, but now I know it was a sympathy "I love you." Do you want to go swimming? I'm sure we can find something to put over my cast."

"L.K., I'm trying to make my move on you and you are missing it."

"I'm in a cast, Ben. I'm not exactly in a making out mood."

"Well, I was thinking a little more than making out. L.K., I think we are ready to have sex. It's totally natural for couples to have sex. I thought that I gave you all of the signs. The dress, the gifts, the ambiance? Did any of that give you a clue?"

"Oh…well, I'm not that bright," I say as Sam and Lynsey pull in and race after us. Thank you!!!

"There you guys are!" Lynsey gasps.

"Oh, hey," Ben says sighing with frustration.

"We were looking for you guys. It's really late. What were you doing out here? Looks like you were having a nice night," Sam says with a smile and a wink at me.

"We were," Ben says.

"Oh, sorry. Well, since we're out here…Lynsey, you want to swim?" Sam asks in her direction.

"Sure. We'll get out of your way," Lynsey says to us.

"Oh, you are not bothering us. Go ahead and swim. I think we were just going to relax and listen to the waves," I say.

"Yeah, relax," Ben says in disappointment.

Sam and Lynsey ran out into the ocean and Ben pulls his arm around me and whispers, "Later." Okay, I thought Ben understood about my life and my standards. I have values and morals! I can't just have sex with him! At least Sam bought me some time. I watch Lynsey and Sam play in the water. The sounds of the waves are so soothing.

When we got back to the suite, Ben carried me into my room. He sat on my bed while I went into the bathroom to change into my long sleeve shirt and pajama pants. I look at myself in the mirror. Good, I don't look attractive at all. I open the door and flop on the bed.

"Sorry," he says.

"For what?"

"Our night got so screwed up. Every time I plan a special night everything gets messed up. First with James, then Jennifer, then your foot, and Sam and Lynsey. I'm so sorry. I wanted us to have a special night."

"Ben, it was special. We don't have to have sex to have a special night."

"What do you mean?"

"I don't really think we need to have sex."

"I don't know if I can have a relationship without it."

"What are saying? You don't want to be with me?"

"I do, but I would like for us to be more physical."

"Relationships are not built on just the physical. What do you think?"

"I guess that works for some people. I don't think I'm going to change my mind though. I'm all about the sex and you are too hot."

He kisses me and puts his hand on my bare stomach. Okay, I feel totally breezy now and not in a good way. He brushes his fingertip across my breast and then down to my stomach again. He cannot go there! This is not Strip Tease. I grab his finger and kiss it. "Good night, Romeo," I say.

"Good night, Sweetie. We'll talk tomorrow. Are you sure you don't want to?"

"Ben, please try to understand where I'm coming from."

"I'll try. So, are you ready for the party?"

"Yep. Hey, this week has been the first time that we have had actual conversations and been able to see each other. It was nice."

"Yeah, it was. Night." He shut my door and I feel like he shut the door to us. I don't know what's going to happen, but I hope that he can move past this obstacle. Thank you, God for keeping me sane and true to myself!

Friday! I can't believe the party is here! I hope the Finns are all set for the party and I hope Storm remembers this birthday because it is going to be awesome! I can't wait to get paid. I need some shopping money. I hope I get a bonus again.

Ben hasn't said anything to me at all this morning. He kissed my cheek and took his coffee back to his bedroom. Lynsey walks in the kitchen dancing and singing. "What is up with you?" I ask.

"I am packed and ready to go home. I cannot wait to get back to New York."

"Oh, me too. I cannot explain to you how bad I want to go home. I think Ben is mad at me because I wouldn't have sex with him. It totally sucks! You know I don't rock like that."

"I know you don't. Maybe it will all blow over," she says.

"Or blow up." I shrug my shoulders and go back to my room. I pack all of my bags and flop on the bed. Ben opens the door and sits beside me. "Well, are you ready to go home?"

"Totally. I am all packed and ready to go. I'm ready to go back to work. What time are we leaving?"

"Well, I figured we could leave the party early enough to pick up our bags and take off. Is that okay?"

"Cool with me. Where is Sam?"

"He went swimming."

"Oh. So, are we okay?"

"Sure. I need to think, but we are okay."

"Okay." I kiss him and decided to take a nap before the party. Wearing a cast can sure take it out of you. I put my head on Ben's lap and try to fall asleep. I keep thinking about last night. Is Ben going to break up with me? Am I going to lose my job? Will I have to pay for my own ticket back home? What's for lunch? I can't sleep with so much on my mind.

I decide to skip the nap and eat. I'm starved and that party doesn't start for hours. I grab my crutches and hobble to the kitchen. "Why do we have no food?"

"I think Sam and Lynsey have been eating a lot of late night snacks," Ben says.

"Huh, well, I guess I can order Chinese. Egg rolls are always good." I grab my cell and call the nearest restaurant.

"Hello. This is Hunan's. May I take your order," the Chinese man says. I once ordered Chinese and a Mexican man took my order. I find that ironic that a Mexican man was working for a Chinese restaurant. "Hello?" he says. Oh, Crap! I totally lost my thought.

"Oh, hello. I would like to order Chicken Fried Rice, Mongolian Beef, Egg Rolls, and Wontons. Oh, and can I have some of those yummy, little donuts with the sugar on the top?"

"Yes. So, I have an order of Chicken Fried Rice, Mongolian Beef, Egg Rolls, Wontons, and donuts? And then?"

"No and then. That will be all."

"And then I need your address."

"Oh, yeah!" I give him the suite address and then call room service.

"May I help you?" a woman answers.

"I would like to order some chicken," I say.

"What kind of chicken?"

"Strips, nuggets, anything."

"If you don't specify, I'll bring all of it."

"Okay, strips then."

"I'll send them right out." With that, she hung up. How rude! Angry, room service lady. No tip for you. I hope she doesn't bring me my chicken. She might kill me for ordering it. Maybe I'll let Ben answer the door. Don't want to take any chances.

"Why did you order chicken?" Ben asks.

"I had to order chicken to eat now and save the Chinese for later."

"Why not eat it now while it's fresh?"

"Because I like stale Chinese food. It's better when it's old and has set in all the juices."

"Whatever you say."

The day passed so quickly. It wasn't long until our Limo pulled into Disney World. I tried to wear a dress that covered my cast. I didn't want the Finn's to think that I was incapable of doing my job. Sam and Lynsey insisted on coming along. I think they only wanted free food, but it was nice to have them there.

Mickey and Minnie were in front of the castle waving people into the party and taking pictures will all of the kids. Ben was very quiet on the way. "Hey, you okay?" I ask him.

"Yep. I'm just getting ready to see your work. I hope everything goes okay," he says in a pretty monotone voice. He's still mad at me.

"It should. I made sure we had everything. I have called the Finn's and they are ready too. You have nothing to worry about."

"Well, with your foot, I didn't know if you were on top of it."

"Ouch! Kick me while I'm down, Oscar!"

"Sorry. I'm just ready to get home. Construction on the building started this week. I have had tons of calls and Marge is throwing a fit about having to take care of things."

"You didn't have to come."

"Well, I thought that I'd be getting some this week, but apparently that won't be happening!"

"Okay, you are officially ticking me off! Why don't you go back to the suite and wait for us? I really don't like you right now!" I didn't realize that I was screaming until I notice everyone looking at us.

"Fine! Be back at the suite in one hour! I'm changing our flight plans. We are going home as soon as possible." He starts to stomp off and I hobble over to him.

"Stop, I'm sorry. Please stay."

"I'm sorry too, but I think I want to be alone before we leave. I'm just not in the mood for a Disney party." He kisses my forehead and walks back to the Limo.

"Hey! Wait! I don't want to go to the party either," Lynsey said.

"What?" Sam looked at her.

"I kind of wanted to pick up a few souvenirs."

"You can get those at the airport," Sam says.

"I know, but I just don't want to go to the party, but you can stay. You can help L.K. with her crutches. You be her date. I totally don't care. You two are friends and I know that."

"Are you sure?" I ask.

"Yep. See you in a bit," she tells us. She kisses Sam and follows Ben into the Limo.

"Okay, that was weird," Sam says.

"Yeah, it was. Well, I guess you are my date for tonight, Prince Charming. You really look nice."

"Thanks, Beautiful!" he says as he helps me into the party. He has never called me beautiful before. It was kind of nice. I can't help thinking that the best moments on the trip have been with Sam.

The Finn's meet us at the door. I introduce myself, "Hey! I'm Lora Kate London, your party planner."

"Oh, Ms. London! This party is wonderful! Storm is having a blast dancing with all of the princesses. Thank you for taking your time to make sure everything goes okay tonight!" Mr. Finn yells. It's really loud in here.

"I can only stay for an hour. Our flight was earlier than we thought. I should be here to make sure the performers are ready."

"Oh, that's perfectly fine! We are just glad that you are here. You are officially part of the Finn family now. We are going to send you a great bonus. Everything is just perfect."

"Wonderful, but you don't have to do that."

"Storm is having a blast and you deserve it. Besides, Grandpa is paying for it!"

"Well, thanks!"

"Have a good night and thanks again!" They walk off to talk to other people.

"Hey, that's great!" Sam yells.

"I know. I love this job!"

We go behind the stage to see if everything was ready. High School Musical was dressed and ready. They all looked so nervous. You would think that people who do this for a living wouldn't get nervous, but I guess we all have weaknesses. Miley Cyrus is so pretty. She is totally nice too.

"Hey, this is nice," Sam says.

"What?"

"The party, of course."

"Oh, yeah?"

"Yeah! I think you have found your calling!"

We went into the kitchen area. There is some serious cooking going on in here. They are all scrambling around making sure there is enough food. I look over at the table and see the cake, the glittery castle cake. Glittery icing. I'm still amazed with that.

"Does that cake have glittery icing?" Sam asks.

"Yeah, isn't that cool?"

"You and cake. Will you get to take some home?"

"Probably not. We have to leave in 30 minutes."

"I can't believe Ben changed our flight. He must be really mad."

"Well, he shouldn't be. I shouldn't have to give up my morals for anyone. Let's go check on Storm and then we can leave."

"Okay."

Storm was surrounded by her friends when her dad got on stage and introduced High School Musical and Miley Cyrus. Her face lit up and the whole place filled with screams. "I guess that means they like it," I say.

"I can't believe you have pulled off two great parties with top notch performers and caterers. You are going to be famous one day," Sam says giving me a hug.

"Thanks. Well, we better take off. Ben will be mad if we are late."

"We cannot leave until you have a picture with Mickey and Minnie."

"What? No."

"Yes." He pulls me and asks the photographer to take my picture with Mickey and Minnie.

"You are going to take it with me." I hobble over and sit beside Mickey with Sam next to Minnie.

"Okay, get ready," the photographer says.

Sam pulls me close and kisses my cheek when the lady snaps the camera. "Yuck!" I wipe away the kiss and we grab our picture.

We took a cab back to the suite. I hate cabs! Now that I have been in a Limo all week, I don't like cabs at all. They smell and the drivers are creepy.

The driver pulls into the suite and Sam helps me out of the cab. We open the door and all of the lights are out, but I hear some noises coming from one of the bedrooms. "What is that?" I whisper.

"I don't know. Let's go check it out."

Sam and I slowly open the door and turn on the light. Oh, my gosh! Ben and Lynsey are having a sex! They both turn their heads over towards us. "I can't believe this!" I hurl one of my crutches at them! "I am so mad! This is ridiculous! I guess since I didn't put out you found someone who would!" I look over at Sam. He is just standing there staring. "What is wrong with you?" I scream at him.

"Get mad!" He must be in shock or something because he picks up the crutch that I threw and left.

"L.K., I...I'm sorry. We didn't mean to fall for each other. It just happened," Lynsey says while putting on her clothes.

"Don't talk to me! Ben, I can't believe this. I thought that you could respect my wishes, but apparently you can't. I can't believe that you slept with my roommate!"

"L.K., I don't know what to say. It just happened. Can we forget this?"

"Are you kidding me? We were not on a break, Ross! I can't be with someone who sleeps with my roommate! From now on, consider us employer/employee. I am no longer your girlfriend. You are disgusting and vile to me! Oh, and Lynsey, get ready to move because you are no longer my roommate. I am immediately evicting you! I can't live with someone who sleeps with my boyfriend!" I hop to the Limo with one crutch and plop down beside Sam.

"Well, that was an interesting book end to a great vacation, huh?" I ask.

"Yep," he said as he hands me my other crutch.

"You okay?"

"You know, I thought that I would be more upset, but I'm not. Lynsey and I…we were not it. She is not the one for me. I'm ready to go back to New York and my job and our lives. Just me and you again."

"Me too."

Lynsey and Ben step into the Limo. Our driver, Tyler, loaded our luggage and climbed into the front seat. "Are we all ready, Mr. Sparks?" he asks.

"Yes."

That was the last word we heard until we reached New York. Everything seemed like a blur on the way home. We all sat in silence on the plane and all the way home. I didn't want to say anything to make it worse. I think everyone was thinking the same thing. I am so angry and hurt. Ben was like the perfect boyfriend with a great job and a great heart, but I guess I was wrong. What's going to happen?

It was like New York was feeling what I felt. It was raining steadily with gloomy clouds covering the night sky. When the Limo pulls up to my apartment, I hobble out while Sam, Ben, and Lynsey follow.

The driver put the luggage into the elevator for us. I sit on my bench in relief. This is such crap! I broke my foot and my boyfriend is sleeping with my roommate. Great!

When the elevator door opens, I limp over to my door. My door. The door to my world where my problems can disappear. I slowly unlock the door and look inside. My apartment. We all fall in and throw our luggage down. "I'm so exhausted."

"Me too," Sam said as he flops on the couch, "I'm so glad to be back on this couch."

Lynsey and Ben were standing in the doorway staring at us. What did they want me to say? It's okay that you two slept together? I don't think so.

"Lynsey, you better start packing. I want you out in one hour. The same amount time it took you to betray me," I say with no emotion. I know that we are supposed to forgive, but it's really hard right now. I'll have to work on that later.

"L.K., I'm so sorry. I didn't know that this would happen. I want to be honest though. Ben and I have been together all week."

"Well, it doesn't make it any better. I want to be nice to you, Lynsey, but I'm having a hard time. I hope you can understand why I'm asking you to leave."

"Yes." She walks over to Sam. I guess she is ready to apologize to him now.

"Can I talk to you?" Ben asks.

"I guess."

"Let me talk. I want to apologize. I have never been with someone who didn't want to have sex. I really liked you, L.K. I could have even loved you in the future. You are a great party planner and very funny. You have shown me a different side of life and I appreciate that. Yes, it was wrong of me to cheat, but can you blame me?"

"Oh, man! What do you want from me? I cannot approve your mistakes! You apparently don't understand what it means to be a boyfriend. You and Lynsey can be together. I don't care, but you have to admit that you were wrong. If not, then you and Lynsey won't last. Don't you understand that it hurts to talk to you right now? It really hurts! I will learn to forgive you, but I can't look at you right now. We have to learn to move past this because you are my boss."

"I'm sorry that this didn't work out. Lynsey, are you ready?" he turns away from me.

"I have to move my stuff out," she sniffs. She's crying. Sam turns on the television and completely ignores her. I guess Friday night really is alright for fighting as the Gilmore Girls would say.

"I'll have my movers come and pack your stuff. Come on. You can stay with me. We'll go get some food," Ben says.

Lynsey slowly walks over to him as he put his arms around her. Is this when they call curtain? Is this when the screen goes black and the credits roll? They walk out together and never look back. Great, now I have to put out another ad for a roommate.

Chapter 17

Sam and I slept all day Saturday. He never left the couch and I never left my bedroom. We ordered lots of pizza and ice cream. I didn't feel like talking and neither did he. I didn't care that he was on the couch. In fact, I was kind of relieved to have someone there just in case I needed to cry. I have cried for the past two days watching sappy movies that make me cry even more. I'm wallowing and I don't care who knows it. Mom called many times. I told her that I had a break up and I just wanted to eat and cry. She kept insisting that I go see her therapist. She totally doesn't get me sometimes, but Sam does.

On Sunday night, I finally emerge from my bedroom only to find Sam cleaning. "What are you doing?"

"Cleaning. I'm healed. I'm fine. I want to go home and get ready for work."

"Are you sure you're okay?"

"L.K., I've been in a slump for two days. I have prayed. I have cried. I have gained like 10 pounds. God has healed my heart and I'm ready to live again and I really need to go to the gym."

"Well, don't you sound confident?"

"I am. L.K., you didn't need him. He did not deserve you and you did nothing wrong. Someone is waiting for you and it wasn't him."

"Who? Who is waiting for me?"

"I'm going home. Call my cell if you need me. Okay?"

"Okay. I'm going to go visit Mrs. Tragger. I know she misses me."

"No more crying, okay?" He tousles my hair and left.

Where in the world did he get his new profound happiness in two days? I drag myself to Mrs. Tragger's apartment. I knock at her door.

"What?" she hollers.

"Open up, Hildie May! I'm home and I'm hungry!"

"L.K.? Is that you?"

"Yes! Open the door!"

"Fine!" she opens the door and hugs me tight.

"Did you miss me?"

"I missed you so much! I went to Bingo and lost and I had to watch Friends alone. It sucked." (I love when old people use the current lingo. It's hilarious!) What happened to your foot?"

I holed up in her apartment for hours telling her about my awful vacation. We watched T.V. and ate Krispy Kreme donuts until she fell asleep. She can stay up pretty late for an old lady. I cleaned up and covered her with a throw before I left. I went to bed to await the glorious morning.

Getting up this morning was very hard. I think I'll wear my jeans with all the holes and a white T-shirt. I don't really care about my appearance right now. I care more about getting coffee. I grab my Joe and off I go to doom! Crap!

The office was cold and busy when I came in. Marge is sitting at her desk with a frantic look on her desk. She is wearing her usual leopard print with big hair. She put her phone down. "Girl, I am so glad to see you. This place has been crazy. How was the vacation? What happened to you? What's with the crutches?"

"It was more like a dramatic soap opera than a vacation complete with a broken foot and a broken heart, but no one died."

"Oh, I'm sorry. What happened?"

"Mr. Sparks..."

"Uh, oh, Mr. Sparks? Boss name."

"Yep. He slept with my roommate and now we are just employer/employee."

"Huh. Well, you better get to your office before our boss walks in."

"True."

I hop to my office and everything is different. My Pottery Barn office stuff is sitting in the corner. In boxes. What does this mean? Maybe he is moving me away from him. That is totally smart. I don't want to be near him. I only want to work for him. I think I'll go check my mailbox. I start to head over to the break room when I run into Lynsey. What is she doing here? Her internship doesn't start yet.

"Oh, hey, L.K." She says as she walks into my office. Why is she going in there?

"Hey, what's going on?"

She flips her hair and looks straight at me. "Oh, I'm decorating my office."

"I didn't think that interns got an office and this is my office."

"Well, I'm not an intern. I'm head planner and this is no longer your office. It's mine." She has got mean girl attitude today.

"I think I'm confused."

"I was told to tell you to check your mailbox."

"Okay." I hobble into the break room and grab the huge stack from my box. I lay my crutches on the floor and start reading. I got my paycheck and my bonus from the party. I also have magazines, a thank you card from the Finns, and a letter from Ben. Oh, Crap! I open the letter:

Dear Ms. London,

I am sad to announce that I will no longer need you here at Party Central Co. I have enjoyed your work and your company. I deeply regret our parting. You will receive a severance check for your work. Please gather your things and leave gracefully.

Thank you,

Ben Sparks

What a jerk! Severance? That sounds like a death which I guess is true. A death of my job. Leave gracefully? What does that mean? I'm on crutches! There is nothing graceful about the way I leave. I'm sick of this! I hop over to Marge and show her the letter.

"Oh, Honey, I'm sorry. I'm really going to miss you. He really is a jerk. I guess that cute little girl is your replacement. That was quick!"

"She's Lynsey. She's the roommate."

"Oh, Girl! I'm going to make her work hard to keep up here. Call me all of the time. Leave me as a reference on your apps."

"Okay. Bye, Marge. It was nice knowing ya!" I give her a tight hug and call Sam. "Come get me."

"What? I'm working."

"Well, I need you to come get me and my stuff. I was fired."

"Fired?"

"Yes! Fired, Sam! Now, come get me!"

"I can't. I go live in like ten. The people need the weather, L.K."

"Fine! Betray me too! See if I care!" I hang up. Crap!

I call a cab and pay the driver to load my crap. This is so crappy! "Hey, can we make a stop at the nearest bakery?"

"It will cost extra," my grubby cab driver mumbles.

"I just want cake! I want to eat an entire cake and cry! Is that okay with you, Mr. Taxi Man?" I wail.

"I guess. I didn't mean to upset you. I just thought you would like to know that it would be extra," he says in his Brooklyn accent.

"Fine. It's fine."

He pulls into the nearest bakery and I got out with my crutches. The bakery was not very busy so I grab a cake and huge cup of coffee. I didn't realize that I had tears running down my face until the cashier asked me if I was all right.

"I have had the worst couple of days. My boyfriend cheated on me with my roommate. My boyfriend was my boss and he fired me. Now I have no boyfriend, no roommate, and no job."

"Ah, Honey, I 'm sorry. I'll have someone take this out for you."

I pay for my cake and my coffee and follow the worker back to the cab. I give the driver more money and he takes me to my apartment. "I'll give you $100 if you carry my stuff upstairs. With crutches, I can't do anything."

"$100?"

"Yep."

"You got it, Lady."

He carries all of my crap to my apartment and I give him the money. I crank some sappy music and grab a fork. I'm eating this whole cake and no one can stop me.

I look over towards Lynsey's room. Empty. There is a note taped to the door. Huh. What is that? I grab and unfold the pink notebook paper.

Dear L.K.,

I would say I'm sorry again, but I have to be honest. I'm not. (I knew it!) *I love Ben. He and I are soul mates.* (I've heard that before) *We belong together.* (Okay, Mariah Carey, we get it!) *We are both terrible, dishonest people.* (Duh!) *We shouldn't have done that to you or Sam. L.K., you belong with Sam. Sam loves you. I knew that even before we were together. We didn't click like you two do. I hope you can forgive us one day. I hope you find a roommate soon.* (Yeah, me too!)

Love, Lynsey

I don't understand. Why does she think that Sam and I belong together? We are friends. That's all, aren't we? Ugh! I don't want to think about that now. I want to eat cake and cry. I want to wallow in my own self pity. I grab my necklace to feel the cross, but it isn't my cross necklace. It's the cake necklace that Ben bought for me. I read the engraving on the back, "A little frosting for my love." Huh!

I carefully unclasp the necklace and hold it out in front of me. What am I going to do with this? I don't want it anymore. It symbolizes a fake relationship.

Well, I didn't eat the whole cake, but I got pretty close. I want my Mom so I stuff the cake necklace in my pocket and take a cab to my parents' house. I left myself inside and flop on the couch. I'm so glad to be home.

"Who's there?" my Dad yells.

"It's me, Dad!"

"Lora Cake, is that you?"

"Yes, Dad!"

"Oh, what are you doing here?"

"Where are you?"

"Um, in the kitchen."

I hobble into the kitchen only to find Mom and Dad naked in the kitchen! "Oh, crap! What are you guys doing? Is this some sort of Rome thing?" I hop quickly back into the living room.

"Sorry, Honey, we just wanted to know what was so great about having sex in the kitchen. It seems like such a fad," Mom says coming in with her robe on.

"Gross."

"What's going on, Lora Cake? You look sad."

"Ben and I broke up."

"Oh, is that all?"

"Mom, this is big. I could have loved him. He was so cute and sweet."

"Oh, Honey, you shouldn't be crying over him."

"He cheated on me with my roommate."

"You got a roommate?"

"Yeah, Mom, like for a while."

"Oh. I still have jetlag. I'm not myself yet."

"I can see that."

"Have you lost weight?"

"Impossible. I have done nothing, but eat. My jeans are a little loose though."

"You look too skinny. You need to eat. I'm going to cook you something special."

Mom made my favorite dinner, Pot Roast with gravy. I couldn't resist, but I did refuse to eat on the table. I will never eat there again. I also had three slices of cheesecake.

"Okay, Mom, I'm better. I'm going to the beach for a while to think. I love you."

"Love you too, Lora Cake."

"Tell Dad I love him."

"I will. You be careful."

"Okay."

I didn't do too bad getting down to the ocean. I only fell twice. I think that I have become less clumsy with crutches. Is that possible? The ocean looks so different here than it does in Florida. It even looks a little sad.

I throw my crutches down on the sand and look at the ocean. I didn't bring my cell with me. I hope I don't get any important calls. Actually, I don't care if I do. I just want to sit here. I pull out the cake necklace and lay it in the sand in front of me.

"Hey, Loser!" Sam's voice scares the crap out of me!

"Don't sneak up like that!"

"Sorry."

"I guess loser would describe me right now."

"You are not a loser."

"Yes, Sam, I am. I let Ben control me and seduce me and cheat on me. It's Jennifer and Brad all over again."

"Lora Kate London! You are not a loser. I'll go beat him up if you want. He made the mistake, L.K. Not you. Angelina and Brad were at fault, not Jennifer and you are not at fault here."

"I know. I don't know why I'm so upset. I knew he was bad for me. I knew that he would end up cheating on me. I knew it."

"What are you doing with that necklace?"

"Debating."

"On what?"

"Whether I should throw it in the ocean or not."

"I say yes."

"It's so pretty though."

"It's your choice."

"Help me up."

Sam pulls me up and hands me my crutches. I look at the necklace one last time. "Well, here goes $50 grand." I chuck it in the ocean as far as I could. "I actually feel better."

"That necklace was $50 grand?"

"Tiffany's."

"We should have sold it."

"That would not make me feel better."

"So, you good now?" he asks as he puts his arm around my waist.

"Yeah, I think I am. You want to go back to my apartment and watch Signs?"

"The old L.K. is back!"

"She was hiding for a while, but she's coming back."

Back at the apartment, Sam and I order pizza, Chinese, and ice cream. "Well, we are ready to eat and watch Signs."

I pop in the DVD and settled on the couch beside Sam. He puts his arm around me. What is with this arm business? I slide over enough for him to move his arm. It feels nice, but weird at the same time.

In the middle of the movie, I decide to move closer to Sam again. It was weird, but it felt safe and normal. I never noticed that he smells like peppermint. He looks at me. "What's up? Are you scared?"

"No. I just couldn't find a comfy spot." I am totally lying! Why am I lying? Do I want to be next to Sam like this? Maybe I do. I think I'll move anyway. I slide over to the arm of the couch.

"Okay, get still. You are jittery."

"Sorry. I can't get comfortable."

The rest of the night was pretty peaceful. I shook the weird feeling. I think it was just a passing thought. I take my crutches and go into my bedroom to change. I pull on an orange nightie. Do I want Sam to see me this way? It was different before because I had a boyfriend and we were just friends. Wait a minute! We are still friends. Just friends. I put on a robe anyway.

"What took you so long?"

"I had to find something to put on."

"You have a million nighties and you couldn't find one?"

"Oh, I found one, but I'm a little chilly (you liar!). I decided to put on a robe."

"It's hot in here. Are you getting sick?"

"Maybe (Maybe I'm crazy). I'm going to bed. You staying here?"

"Yep. I'm lazy and I'm not moving."

"Goodnight."

I hop to my bedroom and take off my robe. I slip into the covers and close my eyes. Yes! Sleep! Before I could drift off, I feel Sam sit beside me so I turn to face him.

"L.K.?" he traces my jaw with his finger.

"Yeah?" That was weird.

"Do you want to go out tomorrow night?"

"Sure."

"Really?"

"Uh, yeah, why would I not? It's not like I have a job to go to."

"I don't know. So you'll go?"

"Yes, but where?"

"I was thinking dinner."

"Okay. You want me to pick up something?"

"No. I want to go out to eat."

"Sure. Call me tomorrow and tell me where and when."

"Nope. I'll pick you up."

"Okay." He is being so strange.

With that he touched my shoulder and left. That was so weird. Am I dreaming? I think I need some coffee to wake me up. Maybe I'll go into the kitchen and brew a pot. Nope! Too lazy. I guess we are going to dinner and he'll pick me up. What is that? Oh, crap! Did he just ask me out on a date?

Chapter 18

The sun, shining through my window, kissed my face. I have a doctor's appointment today. I wish I had Dr. Shad, but I think that ship has sailed. He probably doesn't even remember me. I get dressed in khaki shorts and a light blue polo. I pull my blonde hair into a messy ponytail and grab coffee as I head toward the elevator.

The doors open and there sitting on my bench was James Madden. He is too tall to confront this morning. I don't want him to have the pleasure of being right about Ben. Oh, well, I guess we all have to face the music sometime.

"Good afternoon," I say as I hop in.

"Good afternoon to you! What happened?" he says as he points at my foot.

"The scar of a beautiful vacation."

"Shouldn't you be at work?"

"Shouldn't you be at work? What is work? I've never heard of work."

"You got dumped and fired, didn't you?"

"Yep. He's a cheater. Are you happy? You were right."

"Sorry, London."

"Yeah, me too, but I'll find another job. I'm quite intelligent and gifted apparently. I'll find work."

"I'm sure you will."

"What? No offer?"

"Not today. I'm on vacation."

"Still?"

"Oh, I wasn't on vacation in Florida. I was spying on you."

"You liar!"

"Oh, yeah, I'm a liar. Nice party by the way. I loved the cute, little High School Musical performance and Miley Cyrus? Nice. You didn't stay long though. What happened?"

"Well, Ben and I got into a huge fight. When I went back to the room, he was sleeping with my roommate."

"Huh."

"Wow, I thought I told that story better. It's a pretty big moment in my life. I usually get a pity sigh from my listeners."

"Well, I knew it would happen. I also knew that you would be fine because you're you."

"Thanks, I guess. So, how about a job?"

"Um, I'll have to think about it. Pick up an application at my office and I'll give you a call."

"Are you serious?"

"I told you that I'm on vacation. I don't do work on vacation. You'll have to wait."

"Fine. Play games if you want to, but I play hard, Madden. So, bring it on."

The elevator opened and I give him a little finger wave as I limp to the doctor. I should have taken a cab, but I'm tired of riding in cars. I want to walk in New York City like everyone else. I think I'll get a hot dog on the way home.

The doctor's office is white and full of sick children trying to cough on me. I'm not even sick and I might end up leaving with the Bird Flu or something. What is the Bird Flu? Why would they call it that if people could get it too? And what about Chicken Pox? They really need to do something about these names.

"Loralei Katherine London?" the nurse calls my name.

"That's me." I grab my crutches and follow her into a tiny room with the paper bed.

"Dr. Thatch will be with you in a few minutes," she says as she leaves.

I don't know why they say that. I know the doctor will not be here in a few minutes. He will be here in 30 minutes. Those nurses are paid to say that. I know all of these things.

I had thumbed through all of the magazines when Dr. Thatch came in. "Hello, Dr. Thatch?"

"Ms. London, how are you?"

"Well, I'm tired of crutches."

"We might be able to help with that. Dr. Gipson mailed your x-rays to me and it looks like a small, tiny fracture. I don't think you really needed a cast, but it did make the healing process go faster. I

263

think we can take the cast off and wrap your foot in a boot. How does that sound?"

"Do I have to use crutches anymore?"

"No. You can walk like normal."

"Sounds perfect."

When I got back to my apartment, I checked the newspaper for roommates. No one. There is not one person in this newspaper that I would want to live with. Smokers, drinkers, students (yuck!), artists, ex-cons, etc. I think I need to find a job that can pay all of the bills. I don't want to live with anyone except maybe a dog. I want to turn that other bedroom into a movie theater room with a projector and a huge screen. Okay, I like that idea. I guess I just need to find a job. I need that application from James's company. Maybe he'll pay me enough to avoid getting a roommate.

I went online and downloaded an application. I love the web. It's so handy! I didn't even have to leave my apartment. I quickly filled it out and faxed it back along with my resume. It's kind of a sad resume, but I knew that James wouldn't care. He knows me.

My cell began playing "Thriller" by Michael Jackson. I knew it had to be Sam. Should I answer it or should I let him leave me a message? I don't know. I guess I should answer it. "Hello?"

"Hey, L.K.!"

"Hey…Sam."

"What's up?'

"Well, I'm sitting in my apartment looking for a job."

"Oh. How was your doctor's appointment?"

"I'm wearing a boot and I don't have a cast or crutches. You know, I was thinking about turning that extra bedroom into a movie theater room. What do you think?"

"I think that's a great idea, but how are you going to pay rent?"

"I think James is going to give me a job. I will just have to make sure that he pays me enough so that I don't have to get another roommate."

"Well, that sounds great! So, a movie theater room, huh?"

"Yep. I'll have to get a projector and big screen. I'm kind of excited. This could be a whole new chapter in my life. I could actually get a party planning job because I'm talented not because I'm pretty."

"L.K., I'm glad that you're happy. It makes me happy for you."

"Thanks!"

"I've gotta go, but I'll see you tonight?"

"Definitely."

He sounds nervous. Is this really a date? "Where are we going?"

"I'll pick you up."

"What should I wear?"

"Anything. Be ready by 6:00. Bye."

He hung up. Why is he being so mysterious? This is so weird. What am I going to wear? Should I stay in my jeans or should I dress up? I'm torn. I really need a bath. A big bubble bath with candles and tinkly music.

As I step into the tub, I slide down into the water. This is heaven. This is what I have wanted to do since Friday. I let Britney Spears serenade me while I read a novel by Nicholas Sparks. I know that Britney is not really bubble bath music, but I am too lazy to put a different CD in.

An hour later, I stepped out of the tub and put on my robe. What am I going to wear? I don't want to wear jeans and he takes me to an expensive restaurant. I also don't want to wear a dress if we go to the beach or something. Ugh! I grab my True Religion jeans and a sparkly silk top. I put on my blue sapphire necklace to match my blue top. All I have to do is wait. Wait for Sam to pick me up for a date. Or a nondate? So weird.

At 6:00 on the dot, there was a knock at my door. When I opened it, Sam was standing holding roses.

"These are for you," he says.

"Wow, thanks." I grab a cup from the cabinet and fill it with water as he follows me in. I stick the flowers in the cup. "Well, I'm ready."

"You look gorgeous."

"Thanks, Sam. You look nice too." He was dressed in jeans (Good!) and a green and white polo. He smells good, really good. This has to be a date because he is wearing the good stuff. "So, Ralph Lauren Polo Sport?"

"How did you know?"

"I have a good nose."

"So, are you ready to go?"

"Where are we going?"

"You'll have to wait and see."

When we walk down stairs, I see a shiny, black Mustang convertible parked in front of my building. I love Mustang convertibles! This is a brand new car. Who bought this car? I want to meet them. Sam walks up to the car and opens the passenger door.

"This is your car?"

"Ever since 4:00 p.m."

"You know I want this car."

"You can drive it whenever you want."

"You know you bought my dream car."

"I know."

"Did you do this to make me jealous?"

"No. I wanted us to enjoy the car."

"Us?"

"Yep! Now put this on." He hands me a scarf.

"Put it where?"

"Over your eyes."

"Over my eyes? What is this?"

"Just put it on. Please don't ruin this. I've been working out the details of tonight all day."

"Okay, okay." I tie the scarf around my eyes. I hate not knowing where I'm going. It reminds me of murder movies when the victim is kidnapped and taken to a secret hiding place. This is when the audience is screaming, "Don't do it!" Like they can actually hear you. "You aren't taking me out somewhere to kill me are you?"

"You watch too many movies."

It seemed like forever before the car stopped. I think I fell asleep. Well, it's hard to stay awake when your eyes are covered.

"L.K.?"

"Can I take this off now?"

"Sure."

I pull the scarf away from my eyes and look around. There are trees everywhere full of pink flowers. There's a bridge crossing over a small, bubbling creek. Where are we? I have never been here before.

"What is this?"

Sam gets out and opens my door. He grabs my hand and leads me over to a blanket in the grass below a huge weeping willow tree. I sit down on the blanket and he sits beside me. "Sam, what is this all about?"

"Let's save the conversation until later. First, let's eat. I brought Pete's pizza and Gray's Papaya hot dogs. Your favorite."

"Sammy, this is so sweet. What's the special occasion? Did you get promoted?"

"Talking later."

"So I can't talk?"

"You cannot ask any questions about tonight."

"Okay, Mr. Mysterious."

We ate the pizza and the hot dogs. I think Sam wants to make me fat. I know that I have a big appetite, but I am stuffed. What I really want to know is what is going on? He is being so cryptic. Ben and I have been broken up for what? A few days? Why would Sam ask me out now? He knows that it's too soon.

The sun was setting. What in the world are we going to do in the dark? Maybe this was it. Maybe we are going to pack up and go home. "So...?"

"Look straight ahead."

"At what? That old shed barn thing?"

"Yeah."

"What about it?" As soon as the words left my lips, I hear a noise behind me and then see a flash of light. I look back at the barn. It's like a drive in movie. It's Breakfast at Tiffany's! I love this movie! "Sam? This is like straight out of Gilmore Girls."

"I remember watching that episode when you said, 'I can't stand Christopher, but I do give him props for one of the most romantic moments ever.' So I thought I would give it shot."

"Sammy? This is..."

"Just sit back and enjoy the movie. I'll be back." He got up and went back to the car. He comes back with pillows and extra quilts. He also has popcorn and Peanut Butter M&Ms. He is being so sweet and extra romantic. I know this is the part where everyone is tilting their heads and saying how sweet it is, but I just don't know. Sam and I are such good friends. Why would we want to ruin it?

I get all comfy and grab a handful of popcorn. I know I said that I was full, but I can't resist popcorn. Even though Breakfast at Tiffany's is one of my favorite movies, I still can't concentrate. Sam looks so nice tonight and he is being romantic. That is a strange word for me to put with Sam. Honestly, I don't know how to feel.

When the movie stops, Sam takes my hand. He better not propose! He looks at me with eyes that I've known forever. His eyes are soft and sparkling. He looks so happy. Do I look the same? Are my eyes all sparkling? Is it too soon to have a relationship? Do I want that relationship to be with Sam? Sam and I have been so close. He makes me happy and he is the sweetest guy I know. He is the most trustworthy guy I know. He is always there to pick me up when I fall. Sam is the first one there when I'm crying or just having a rotten day. But...

"L.K., I wanted tonight to be special. You and I have had a hard week. I wanted you to feel special again. You are the best girl in New York City. Hey, you're the best girl in the world. I care about so much about you. You are my best friend and you will always be special to me."

"Sammy, I care about you too. You didn't have to do this."

"Yes, I did. You deserved it."

"Thanks, Sam. You're the best!" I give him a huge hug. "I really needed this. A night with no problems. This has been so great."

Sam stood up and turned on the radio in the car. "Lucky" by Jason Mraz and Colbie Caillat was playing. I love this song. "L.K., could I have this dance?" Sam asks as he holds out his hand.

"Yes, you may." I'm not sure how well I will dance in this boot.

I take his hand as he pulls me up from the blanket. Sam wraps his arms around my waist. His hands are warm and comforting. As we sway with the music, I feel my body naturally move closer to him like I can't control it.

Sam runs his finger through my hair and I look deeply into his eyes. I don't think I can do this. Sam and I are best friends. We're not a couple. I can't stop the thoughts that flow through my mind. They're all jumbling and getting mixed up. I decide to pull away.

"What's wrong?" he asks.

"I don't know, Sam. Does this feel right?"

"It has always felt right."

"We are best friends."

"That makes it better. Don't you think?"

"Sam, Ben and I just broke up. I need time to heal."

"I understand." His face drops.

I don't want to hurt him. He's too important to me. "Can we talk about this?"

"Sure."

I sit back on the blanket and cover myself with the quilt. Sam sits beside me. "Sam, I really care about you. I just want to make sure that this is real. I have to be honest, I haven't thought of you in a romantic way. I…" He touches my cheek and pulls me close to him. He pulls the stray blond hair away from my eyes and begins to kiss me. I mean like a real kiss. A rush moves through my entire body. His lips are soft and warm. He tastes like Dr. Pepper and peppermint. Okay, that was some kiss. That was a knock-the-breath-out-of-you kiss.

"How is that for real, Lora Kate London?" He stands up and walks over to the car.

"Where are you going?" I grab all of the blankets and hobble over to the car. I stuff them into the back seat as I hop in beside Sam. "You can't just kiss me and then walk away."

"Why not?"

"Who said I wanted just one kiss?" I lean in closer to him and he backs away.

"One special night and one special kiss."

"You are killing me!"

"Sorry, London. You get one kiss. That's it." His smile returns.

We drove home in silence. I don't know what to feel. Should I want to kiss Sam? I don't know if it was him or the moment, but I want to do it again.

He pulls into my apartment building and opens the door for me. I get out and follow him to my apartment. He stops at my door and pulls a tiny box from his pocket. "Only open it if you want."

"You are being so mysterious tonight."

"That was my plan."

"You're not coming in?"

"Not tonight."

"Well, goodnight." I start to give him a hug, but he grabs my hand and kisses it.

"Goodnight." With that he walked away.

What a night! Should I open this box? He wouldn't know if I did or if I didn't. I guess I could open it and if I don't like it, then I'll tell him I didn't open it. I have to open it though, right? Who am I talking to? No one is going to answer me!

I slowly open the box and find a key. The key has a little horse on it. Oh, my gosh! It's the key to the Mustang! I grab my cell and dial his number. "You gave me the Mustang!"

"Look outside."

I hobble downstairs and open the building door. I trip over the rug again and fall flat on my face. They need to get rid of that rug. It's a hazard to my health. When I stand up, there, sitting in front of the building, is the Mustang. "I can't believe this! Why?" I say in the phone.

"L.K., I have to be honest. This is not a gift from me."

"So, you did want to make me jealous!"

"No. The car is from your parents. They bought it for you when they got home from Europe. I was told to surprise you with it. I don't really know why they bought you a car."

"I do. I saw them naked in their kitchen. I bet they bought the car for them and then they felt guilty about me seeing them naked, so they gave me their car."

"You saw them naked?"

"Long story."

"Well, there is a gift from me. Open the glove compartment."

I go over to the car (My car!) and open the glove compartment. There is another tiny box. I'm beginning to love tiny boxes. I open and find a slip of paper. It says, "Go upstairs."

"What is this?"

"Follow the notes," he says and then he hung up.

I go upstairs and there is a note on my door. "Open." I open the door and there are red rose petals scattered all the way to my bedroom door where I find another note. "Get comfy."

I go into my bedroom and find my yellow nightie and robe lying on my bed. I change and find another note on my bathroom mirror. "Make popcorn." Good grief! I find the popcorn and put it in the microwave. I open the cabinet to grab a bowl and find another note. Okay, Sam, how many notes did you write? "Go to the spare room." I grab my popcorn and tiptoe into the spare room. It's dark. What am I supposed to be looking at?

I turn on the light and the room has been completely redecorated. The walls are covered in movie posters like Signs, The Notebook, Twilight, Dirty Dancing, and Grease. There is a huge leather sofa with cup holders facing a huge screen. Oh, my gosh! Sam made my movie theater room!

I sit on the sofa and look at the screen. This is so awesome! There are two huge shelves on each side of the screen full of my DVDs. What am I going to watch first? While I was glancing over all of my movies, someone covers my eyes. "Sam?"

He uncovers my eyes and looks down at me. "Sammy, this is too much," I say.

"Is it?"

"How did you get all of this done?"

"I have my resources."

He sits down beside me and presses play on the remote. I grab the quilt that was draped over the sofa and wrap it around me. "I know you said that I could only have one kiss, but can I sit close to you?"

He opens his arms and I slide close to him. As Sweet Home Alabama plays, he wraps his arms around me and squeezes me close. Being in his arms feels like being in the sun on a warm day. Through the whole movie I can't shake this crazy feeling. Am I falling in love with my best friend?

Chapter 19

When I wake up, I am in my bed. I tiptoe into the bathroom and turn on my shower. The shower feels hot and comforting. Last night was amazing, but it is happening so fast. Does love work this fast? Do I love Sam? We have been friends since college. He's been with me during every break up. He brings me cake when I'm sad and holds me when I cry. I don't know. I just want to get away and take my mind off Sam. My parents bought me a car. I am unemployed and I have nothing to do. I think I'll go shopping with my Visa.

I stay in the shower until my skin is all wrinkly. I put on camouflage pants and a white T-shirt with flip-flops. Well, one of my flip-flops. I grab my Louis Vuitton bag and hit the road. I am going to shop and not think about Sam.

I press the down button on the elevator. When the doors open, I see James sitting on my bench. "Okay, get up. I'm still partly injured and I need the bench."

"Okay, London, I'll give you the bench." He stands up and lets me sit down. This is my bench and I refuse to give it up!

"So, are you still on vacation?"

"Well, I was, but I'm needed at the office. Dolly couldn't handle it on her own. She is my assistant."

"Dolly? Like as in Dolly Parton?"

"No, not Dolly Parton. Dolly Woods."

"That's not much better."

"What do you care?"

"Well, I wanted to make sure that I didn't get my future co-worker's name wrong."

"I haven't hired you."

"But you will."

"Well, I assume that I will have a nice application to look at when I get to the office."

"Why deal with the paper work when you could hire me now?" The doors open.

"Bye, London. I'll call you."

"Okay. Bye, Boss."

"Don't call me that," he says with a smirk.

"Sorry, Boss."

"Ugh!" He walks away, but I can tell he is smiling.

I know that I shouldn't be spending money when I have no job, but my severance pay and my bonus money from the party will cover me for a while. I have to shop today. I don't want to think about Sam. I get into my new Mustang and speed off.

As I walk into the mall, my cell starts ringing. It's Sam. I'm not going to answer. I don't know what I would say. I can't talk to him like I usually would, can I? I decide to turn my phone on silent and go into Old Navy where I buy 3 pairs of jeans, 6 shirts, and a handbag.

I grab a Philly cheese steak for lunch and sit at the last available bench. I stuff all of my bags across from me. I think I've bought something from almost every store. I don't even want to know how much I spent. I check my cell phone. 33 missed calls from Sam. I bet he'll be at my apartment when I get home. Maybe I should just go on like nothing happened and see if things have changed because I don't want things to change. Do I?

I throw all of my bags into the Mustang and start home. I totally love my new car. That reminds me…I need to call and thank my parents. I grab my cell and dial their number. "Hi, Mom."

"Lora Cake, did you like the present?"

"Mom, it's a car! I love it."

"Oh, good. Your Daddy bought it thinking he was going to drive it around, but he saw himself in a building window and realized that he looked like a fat old idiot."

"Okay. Well, I don't really care how I got it. It's just so awesome. This is my dream car."

"I'm glad, Honey Bear. We have some souvenirs for you too."

"Mom, I think the car is enough."

"But that wasn't what I bought for you in Rome."

"Well, I'll get it later. I have a lot to figure out right now."

"Oh, that reminds me. Sam called looking for you."

"He did, huh?"

"Are you avoiding his calls?"

"Kind of."

"Why? Lora Cake, he's so good for you. He watches out for you when we can't."

"I know, but we are friends."

"That is the best kind of man."

"I know, but should he be my boyfriend?"

"Definitely not!"

"What?" I didn't expect that answer.

"He should be your husband!" I didn't expect that one either.

"Mom?"

"Loralei Katherine, you are an adult. You have to make your own decisions, but I am telling you this one time. You need to find someone who will love you and not cheat on you with ditzy girls. You have no job and no boyfriend. Sam told me everything that happened on that awful trip to Florida. I knew I should have taken you with us this summer. You need some stability."

"Mom? I can't believe that you just said that. I'm going to get a job and a boyfriend. In fact, I'm walking in my building right now and I'm sure that Sam is waiting in the living room." I hold the phone with my shoulder while I grab all the shopping bags.

"Well, kiss him and get it over with."

"I'm scared!" Well, there it is. I'm scared to death of falling in love with Sam. I can't admit that to him.

"Well, suck it up!"

"Fine!" I flip my phone shut and fumble with my keys. It's flippin' hard to open a door with a hundred bags.

When I open the door, I stumble and fall over all of my bags. I look up and see Sam giving me a very stern look. "What?" I pull myself up and look at him.

"I called you 33 times. 33 times!"

"Sorry."

"L.K., if you are going to avoid me, I don't see how this is going to work."

"How what is going to work?"

"Our relationship!"

"Last time I checked, you didn't ask me for a relationship. You said one special night and one special kiss."

"L.K., what do you think last night was about?"

"I thought you wanted to make me feel better."

"If I wanted to make you feel better, I would've brought you cake."

"Well, how was I supposed to know?"

"Lor, I was romantic and sweet."

"I know."

"We kissed."

"I know."

"Well?"

I throw my hands up. "I liked it, okay? Are you happy now?"

"Yes, L.K., I'm happy. I'm happy with you. I want to be happy with you forever."

"Well, I'm scared!"

"What are you so scared of? That you might love me?"

"Yes!" I run into my bedroom and slam the door! Did I just tell him that I love him? Oh, geez! I turn the lock on the door. He is not coming in here.

"L.K.?" He jiggles the handle.

"Nope!"

"Open the door! We have to talk."

"No, we do not! I'm not talking to you." I can't deal with this right now. It's too much!

"You love me, but you are not talking to me?"

"That's right."

"Are you serious?"

"Well, I'm not doing stand up."

"Lord, please talk to me."

"I'm afraid that's not possible at this moment."

"Ugh! Call me later!" I hear footsteps and a door slam.

Good he's gone. I can't face him like this. I didn't want to get into this today. I want to look at all the stuff I bought and I want to be by myself tonight. Maybe I'll exercise or bake. I hate both of those things. I just want to be alone or maybe call James and harass him about a job. That'll be fun.

I make a pot of coffee and turn on the T.V. just for some background noise. Whatever happened to Everwood? It was such a good show. It's like it fell off the face of the earth. I finally find Twister. That movie scares me to death. I'm so glad I live where it snows and not where those things are. Tornadoes are creepy.

I think I want to cook something. I really want some pasta, but the last time I tried to cook pasta, I ended up having to throw out my pan and buy a new stove. I don't know if I can afford a new stove right now. I open my cabinets and find nothing. So, I order Pizza.

I eat my pizza in the bathtub. I know that usually people don't eat in the bathtub, but I am not everyone else. I am who I am and I eat pizza in a bubble bath while watching a movie. I have a flat screen built in the wall in the bathroom. I bought it when I was making money. Money. That was nice to have. I actually bought it because Sam suggested it. He said it would be totally worth the investment. I think I agree. This is pretty cool. I prop the pizza box on the corner of the tub and flip the T.V. on to finish Twister.

I can't concentrate. Well, apparently I feel something for Sam. I know that I care about him. I guess I have to admit that Lynsey was right. Sam loves me and I'm perfect for him. I know that's why I could never see those two together. Oh, no, it's all coming to me now. I know exactly why I hated seeing Lynsey with Sam. It's because I wanted to be with Sam. I do want to be with Sam. Life never ceases to surprise me.

After two hours in the tub, I get out and call James. I can't go without messing with him. It's too fun. "Hello."

"This is James. I'm not here right now, but please leave a short message with your name and number and I'll call you back. If this is L.K., hang up. I'll call you."

How rude! I think I'll go give him a little visit tomorrow afternoon. I'm going to get that job. I guess I'll call Sam. I can't completely shut him out. He's probably sitting at home pouting and whining like Linus and watching the phone while eating chips. I dial his number. One ring.

"You ready to talk?" he asks.

"Yes."

"Do you love me?"

"Do I have to answer that again?" I ask.

"I want to make sure that I heard you right."

"You did."

"So, are we…?" he asks. Night of the twenty questions.

"Is that what you want?"

"What do you want?"

"Me. I want to know one thing."

"What is that?"

"Will you let me watch whatever I want?"

"Of course."

"Then, we are."

"We are…together?"

"Do I have to spell it out?" I exclaim.

"No, I just want to know that you are being totally serious with me right now?"

"I am. I didn't want to admit it to myself, but being with you is all I've ever wanted I think. It's still so fresh right now. I can't wrap my mind completely around this yet. Seeing you with Lynsey was so hard for me, but I couldn't really see why until now."

"I thought that being with Lynsey would help me move on from you. When you got that job, which I knew you would, I was so scared. I knew that guy would know how to sweep you off your feet. I knew he would play you, but I just had to tell myself to leave it alone. Lynsey was never really right for me. I spent most of time talking about you."

"No wonder she knew you loved me."

"She did?"

"Yeah. At first, I thought she was crazy. But I can see she was right."

"She was."

"So...well now that you're my boy...friend, I guess that means that you should bring me breakfast in the morning?"

He says, "I do that anyway."

"Well, then I guess you'll have to kiss me when you bring me breakfast."

"I guess so." I can tell that he's smiling.

"Now don't forget the breakfast part. That's the important one," I say with a smile.

"Of course. I'll see you in the morning."

I lay my phone beside me. So, I guess Sam and I are...together. Who knew? Sam and I do belong together. I turn off the lights and fall into bed in my purple nightie. I pray to keep my sanity and close my eyes. My cell phone blings to tell me I have a text. I open the phone and press read. "I love you, Lora Kate London." From Sam. He is so sweet. I text him back, "I love you too."

Chapter 20

I wake up this morning covered in rose petals. What in the world? I look over and there is a long-stem rose on my pillow with a note attached. I open the little envelope and pull the card out, "I am going to love loving you. Have a great day! Sam." Where has he been hiding all this romance? He usually farts on me as a good morning. I like this new side.

 I get dressed in my best outfit, my Escada mini. I put on my heels (I'm not wearing the boot. It looks weird and my foot feels fine.) and lock the door. I'm going to Madden Party Co. and I'm going to follow James around until he gives me a job. I have to get a job. My bills need to be paid and I'm not asking my parents for money. They will make me move in with them and there's nothing in this world that can make me move back there. I don't want to see them naked again. Eww!

I park my 'Stang (I love saying that) around the back of James's building. I don't want him to see me come in. He can't know that I'm here or he'll try to hide.

I walk into the lobby. My old job didn't have a lobby. This is nice. There is a beautiful marble fountain in the front. The floors are even marble. As I keep walking, I find nice offices and cubicles with people walking everywhere. I don't think anyone even knows I'm here. All of a sudden I run smack into a lady with a bunch of papers. "Crap! I am so sorry!" I bend down to help her.

"What are you doing? Who are you?" she asks as she gathers her papers.

"Well, I'm Lora Kate London. I'm here to see James."

"Are you a relative?"

"No."

"Then, you want to see Mr. Madden. He does not go by his first name at the office. Do you have an appointment?"

"Well, not really. See, I need a job and he has one to give me."

"But you have no appointment?"

"Right."

"Then you have no job. Mr. Madden only sees people if they have an appointment."

"Well, James...I mean Mr. Madden and I are sort of friends."

"Oh, well, if you are friends...No! He will not see anyone unless they have an appointment. Sorry!" She stomps away.

Ugh! How rude! He will see me. Now I'm on a mission. I walk frantically around and finally find his office on the top floor down a long hallway. Good grief, his office is hidden well. A lady with big blond hair and big boobs (Okay, this must be Dolly. I can see that.) She is sitting at a desk and has a headset on typing like a mad woman. I move in really close so that she could see me.

She looks up and takes off her headset, "Do you have appointment?" Her accent is very southern.

Why does everyone keep asking that? "No, but James...Mr. Madden will want to see me."

"I doubt it. Mr. Madden is with someone right now. You will have to wait."

"Can do!" I walk over and plop down on the big, black, leather sofa. There is a flat screen in the wall playing MTV. At least I'll have something to do. I wonder if there is a remote to this thing. I search around and can't find one. Oh, well.

An hour later, James walks out of his office. He looks at me and shakes his head. "What are you doing here?"

"I'm here for my job."

"There is no job here. My office is full and I haven't reviewed your application yet. When I do, I will have my assistant call you for an interview. Until, then…there is no job. Now, I have a meeting in five minutes. I have to go. I'll review your application this afternoon."

"That's okay. I can wait."

"Go home and enjoy unemployment."

"You know, I'm pretty comfortable here. I think I'll order in some lunch and watch T.V. Where is the remote to this thing?" I point to the TV.

"You can't stay here. You can't order lunch here. You have to go."

"I'm good...really. I think I'll just wait until this afternoon. I'm getting to know your assistant since we will be working together so much."

"Ugh! You are impossible!" He walks away, but I can tell he is smiling.

"Okay, who are you?" the lady asks.

"I'm Lora Kate London, but you can call me L.K."

"I'm Dolly Woods."

"Nice to meet you, Dolly."

"You are somethin' else. No one talks to Mr. Madden that way. He likes it real professional 'round here. On casual Fridays we can wear jeans, but we can't wear tennis shoes. Mr. Madden thinks that tennis shoes are too casual for the office."

"Too casual? Can you wear flip flops?"

"Only if they are leather."

"Wow, he is strict."

She drawls, "Well, he likes you. You just hang out on that couch over there and relax. This is going to be a fun day. Here's the remote." She hands me the remote and gets back to work.

"Hey, Dolly, where are you from?"

"Tennessee."

"Cool." I knew it!

I flop on the sofa and begin to channel surf. This place is awesome! It's a lot better than Party Central. A lot more money and professionalism. I think I'm going to like it here.

Around two hours later, James walks past me. He slowly turns around. "Why are you still here?" he says.

"I'm waiting until you review my application."

"I don't have time for this. I have a dozen meetings today. I can't review your application today. I'm sorry."

"Give me five minutes and you won't have to review my application."

"I don't have five minutes. My only free time is lunch and I'm not working during my lunch."

"How about we lunch together and we could talk then?"

"Fine. I have lunch at the diner across the street. Meet me there at 12:30."

"I'll see you there."

He marches to his office and slams the door. I love bugging him. He is really getting mad and I love it. I decide to call Sam. I haven't talked to him since last night. "Hello." He sounds mad.

"What's up?"

"Oh, hey. I am getting stuff ready for the crew tonight. There is a major storm system coming in and everyone is nuts here. What are you doing?"

"I'm trying to get a job. James is going to meet with me at lunch."

"Let me guess. You annoyed him endlessly until he gave in."

"You know it!"

"So, did you get my note this morning?"

"Yes and thank you."

"You're welcome. You want to do something tonight?"

"Maybe. Like what do you want to do?"

"I was thinking dinner and maybe dancing. What do you think?"

"I think I'll wear something pretty."

"You always look pretty."

"Oh, geez."

"See you tonight."

"Bye, Sammy," I flip my phone shut and find a good movie.

I look over at Dolly. She is working so hard. I haven't seen her look up since the last time we spoke. She's really nice. I kind of miss Marge though. She was tough and didn't take crap from Ben Sparks. Maybe I can be the Marge of Madden Party Company.

At 12:00, I run over to the diner. It's really small, but I like it. It has a little charm with old license plates hanging on the walls and a jukebox in the corner. I find a booth and grab the menu. This is my kind of place with burgers, onion rings, and the best of all, pie. Any place with pie is all right with me. My cell phone is buzzing. Good grief! "Hello."

"Lora Kate?"

"Yes, Mom?"

"Do you and Sam want to come for dinner?"

"Um, well, I don't know. I think we have plans for tonight. Wait a minute! How did you know about me and Sam?"

"I know everything. Plus, his mother called me this morning to tell me the news."

"He told his mother?"

"Well, at least someone knew. Why didn't you call me?"

"I was going to."

"Sure. Well, we'll have to set a date. I want Sam to feel like part of the family."

"Mom, we aren't getting married."

"Well, maybe one day."

"Um, I don't think so. I'm not into the whole marriage thing right now. I want to live and let live."

"Oh, Lora Kate, I wish you would settle down. I need some grandchildren."

"Maybe one day. I've got to go. My lunch date is here."

"You have a date and you are with Sam?"

"It's not a date. It's a job interview."

"Oh, good, if you don't get a job, Daddy is moving your stuff over here to our house. We've tried our best letting you live on your own, but we are concerned."

"Bye, Mom." I hang up. She is so paranoid.

James walks up to the booth and sits down. "Okay. Let's order and talk."

The waitress comes over to the table and James orders, "I'll have a double cheeseburger with everything and cheese fries. I want iced tea with lemon and I will want my usual cherry pie also."

"I'll have the same," I say.

"Wow. I didn't know there was a woman in New York City who had an appetite. Most women around here are stick pole thin and never eat. It's disgusting."

"Oh, I can eat."

"Well, let's get down to business, London. You want a job. Why should I hire you?"

"Well, I'm good at what I do."

"Can I trust you?"

"Of course."

"I've seen your work and I have to say that I'm impressed. I do need someone to help me."

I look at him in shock. "Are you getting rid of Dolly?"

"No, she's great. I need someone to plan parties and be in charge at the same time. I have an office in L.A. and I need someone to head up things there. The boss there quit on me. Too much work. L.A. parties are big. Lots of celebrity events. What do you think?"

"Of what? Moving to L.A.?"

"Yeah. I have an office in Paris too. It's good money. So?"

"Oh, James, I don't know. That means moving away from my family and Sam."

"Sam?"

"He's kind of my boyfriend, I guess."

"You already have another boyfriend?"

"Yes, don't judge."

He laughs a big belly laugh. "I'm not judging."

The waitress brings our food and refills our drinks. "Can I have some time to think about it?"

"Sure. I can give you a couple of days to decide."

"A couple of days…okay."

Wow….L.A. I've never thought of leaving home to get a job. I guess California could be great, but do I want to leave? What about Sam? Will he want to follow me to L.A.? What about the earthquakes? I have a lot to think about. I didn't expect him to offer me a job in L.A. I really need a job, though. I guess I could take the job and then tell Sam. I see a fight in the forecast. I think I'll give it a couple of days.

After lunch, it began to thunder and rain. Crap! That's all I need. I go home in kind of a shock. I honestly didn't expect James to put me in charge of anything. I expected a job at maybe getting coffee and lunch for people, but a top job in Los Angeles? What will Sam say? Will he want to follow me to L.A.? I wouldn't blame him if he didn't. What am I going to do?

When I get home, I order ice cream. Ice cream solves all problems. It has magic in it or something. When people break up, they eat ice cream. Then, all of a sudden, they have found someone new. It's the ice cream. I change into jeans and a tank top. I might as well get comfortable. My foot is throbbing. I knew I should have worn my boot. Now my foot is going to swell.

Sam opens the door to find me going through my second pint of Ben and Jerry's and an ice pack on my foot. I don't want to tell him what's going on. Our relationship just started. I can't just ask him to up and move because I was offered a new job, can I?

"You are eating ice cream. I guess that means no dancing. Okay, what's wrong? You only eat ice cream like that when something's wrong. Oh, crap, did he not offer you a job?"

"Oh, he offered a job alright."

"That's great!"

"Not exactly."

"Okay, L.K., tell me what's wrong." Sam takes the ice cream out of my hand and puts his arm around me.

"Well, he offered me a big job. A job that would be great for me. A job that would be a million times better than the one I had. It would be more money, better benefits, and I would be in charge."

"Okay, I don't see what is so bad."

"It's in Los Angeles."

There is a moment of silence. He just stares at me without saying a word. I knew he would be upset. He's probably thinking of a way to break up with me right now. Okay, I can't take the pressure. I have to hear something. "Sam?"

"Okay, I have to think." He gets up and walks to the kitchen table.

I walk over and touch his shoulder. He removes my hand and faces me. He has tears in his eyes. What in the world? I haven't even told him that I didn't take the job yet. He is jumping to conclusions. "Sammy..."

"I can't believe this! Everything was perfect and now you are going off to L.A. to work for some guy!"

"Sam! I didn't take the job!"

"What?" he asks as he wipes his eyes.

"I didn't take the job yet."

"Yet?"

"Well, I wanted to discuss it with you first."

"What is there to discuss? You got a job. You have to move. It was nice knowing you." He grabs his keys and heads for the door.

"Sam! Wait!"

"Wait for what, L.K.? Wait for you to dump me? No thanks! I'm dumping you first!"

"You're dumping me?"

"Yes!"

I follow him down the stairs barefoot into the rain with my foot throbbing. I am getting completely soaked. This is ridiculous. "Sam! Please stop!"

"What? What do you want from me? I gave you everything. I gave you my entire heart and you just stomped on it." I can barely see him through the sheets of rain.

"Sam, I didn't take the job."

"You said that you didn't take the job yet, which means that you are going to take it later. I can't have a long distant relationship with you. I can't go one day without seeing your beautiful face or hearing your sweet voice. L.K., I love you. If you want to move to L.A., that's fine, but you won't be with me. I love you, but I'm not going to have a relationship with you if you go to L.A."

"Sam, I want you to move there with me. We could get two apartments in the same building. You could be the weatherman for California."

He looks confused as he says, "You want me to move?"

"Well, if you want to. If you want to stay here, I'll tell James to find someone else." My teeth are chattering. It's freezing out here.

"You want me to move?"

"Haven't we already been there?"

"You would give up the job for me?"

"Well, yeah, I love you, duh!"

He pulls me close and gives me another one of those amazing firework kisses. It's just like Ross and Rachel in front of Central Perk. I love having a boyfriend that loves me. He scoops me up and carries me upstairs.

I give him a towel to dry off while I change in my bedroom. I lock the door and strip. Did I just tell Sam that I would give up my job offer? Oh, crap! I don't want to give up my job. I need that job or I'm going to be evicted. I change into my flannel sheep pajamas. I know that its summer, but I'm freezing.

I walk into the living room and find a note on the door. "Went to change into dry clothes. Take a bath and relax. I'll bring dinner. Love, Sam."

Good! Now I can think and pray. Maybe God and I can come up with some way to fix my job situation. I run my bath water and pour in bubbles and bath salts. I light all of my candles and slide into the tub. I cannot believe the summer I've had. The new job, the roommate, the boyfriend, my parents, Gerta, James, Bingo, the new boyfriend. I don't know where my life is going, but I know that everything has worked out for the good. I guess this will too.

I hear a knock at my bathroom door. "Sam?"

"Hey, I brought Italian. Are you coming out any time soon?"

"I'll be there in a second." I grab a towel and blow out my candles.

I put my pajamas back on and meet Sam in the movie theater room where he had arranged the spaghetti, the breadsticks, salad, and chicken strips. I know that chicken strips are not Italian food, but I have to have them when I eat spaghetti. Don't ask.

"Wow, nice set up," I say as I grab a bunch of everything from the bar, which contains Dr. Pepper, my fave.

"Well, it's a special occasion."

"What's that?"

"Your new job."

"But I thought that..."

"I wonder if California can handle this weatherman."

"What?" I smile.

"Well, I just hope there is a job for me. You know the sun shines all of the time there, right?"

"I thought that you wanted me to decline."

"L.K., I just want to be with you. I don't care where that is. I'm going to miss New York, but I would be miserable without you. You are everything to me. I can live without Pete's pizza, Broadway shows, and Central Park, but I can't live without you."

I bite my lip. "Sammy, are you being serious right now?"

"As long as you give me time to plan. I need a new job and we need to find two apartments."

"I can't believe this. I mean, normally, this wouldn't happen to me. Normally, I'd be dumped and left standing in the rain. It's like a sappy, love movie."

"Does that mean you're happy?"

"Yes, I'm happy. Very happy." I wrap my arms around him and snuggle close to his side.

The rest of the night went pretty well. I spilled spaghetti all over the front of my pajamas, but that's normal. Sam went home around 1:00 a.m. and I fell asleep on the couch.

Chapter 21

When I woke up, I was on the floor and sweating. What was I thinking? Flannel pajamas in the summer? I went to my bathroom and peeled my pajamas off. Good grief! I took a quick shower and then made coffee.

I decide to call James. I can't wait to tell him I'll take the job.

"Madden Party Company, this is Dolly. How may I direct your call?"

"Hey, Dolly. This is L.K."

"Oh, hey, I heard about your new job offer."

"How did you hear?"

"News travels fast 'round here. Someone ate lunch near ya'll yesterday and spread it everywhere. You are the top story this mornin'."

"Cool! Could you get Mr. Madden for me?"

"Sure, Baby Doll." I hear a click and then a ring.

"This is James Madden."

"Madden, I'll take it."

"Is this you, London?"

"Who else would it be?"

"So, you'll take the L.A. job?"

"That's what I'm saying. I need two weeks though."

"Two weeks? What for?"

"Sam needs to find a job."

"You mean your boyfriend is going to follow you to L.A.?"

"Yep."

"Huh, well, I can give you one week. I can't give you two because I'll need to go with you to L.A. and show you the ropes of the business and I can't leave the office after two weeks. I have a ton of meetings and I am interviewing with someone to head up my Paris office. You will be the boss in L.A. Can you handle it?"

"Do you think I can handle it?"

"I wouldn't have asked if I thought you couldn't."

"So, you are interviewing with someone for the Paris job, huh?"

"Yep."

"Is it a woman or man?"

"What does it matter?"

"Well, I just want to know my competition."

"L.K., you will both be working for me."

"I know, but I want to out do them," I say rubbing my hands together.

"It's a man."

"Oh, great. Does he speak French?"

"That's part of the requirement."

"Oh, geez, a bilingual. That's all I need."

"Do you want to meet him?" he asks.

"No. Not yet anyway. Wait until I'm successful and then we'll meet."

"I'll call you later and give you details. I'll let you spend today finding a place to live and pack, but you're my employee, Missy, and you have to be here tomorrow at 8:00 a.m. sharp."

"Yes, sir!" I hang up and dial my parent's house.

"Hola, London residence." Okay, she is having trouble getting out the words.

"Who is this?"

"Maria Sanchez, who is this?"

"This is Mr. and Mrs. London's daughter, Lora Kate. May I speak with them?"

"Si, uno momento." Okay, I don't know Spanish. I'm going to assume that meant yes.

"Hello," Dad and Mom said at the same time. Oh, good grief, they are using the speaker phone.

"You guys don't have to answer together."

Mom says, "Oh, it's you. I heard about your new job."

"How did you know?" For this to be a big city, news travels way too fast.

"Brandy, your cousin, works at the diner that you had lunch in and she called me."

"Who?"

"Your cousin, Brandy. Minnie's daughter."

"Again, who?"

"My distant cousin on my mother's side, Minnie."

"I have no idea who that is."

"Well Minnie and Brandy go to every reunion. You should know them."

"I never go to the reunions. How do they know me?"

"Well, you should go to some. Anyway, you should take the job," she says. I can hear Dad grunt in the background.

"Well, that's good because I already took it."

"You didn't consult with us first."

"Mom, you just said that I should take the job."

"Well, I didn't think you took it. Brandy said that you told the man that you would think about it."

"I did think about it." She is forgetting that I'm an adult.

"What about Sam? Doesn't he get a say so in this?"

"Mom, Sam and I are both moving to L.A."

Dad pipes in, "Not in the same house, I hope." Now he chimes in.

"No, Daddy, we are getting two separate apartments."

"Well, that's alright then."

"I'll call you both later."

"Bye, Honey."

I flip my phone shut and slide onto my big comfy couch. Sam is finding our apartments. I already have my job. I have my coffee. I'm good. I can't believe everything is happening so fast. Hey, I'm on a roll. I might as well call Sam and see if he has found anything.

"Hey, Cake, what's up?" he asks.

"Well, I was wondering how it's going?"

"Well, I think I found somewhere for us to live."

"Yeah?"

"Yep, two apartments right next to each other."

"Where is it?"

"In Los Angeles," he jokes.

"Oh, geez. What about a job?"

"I have e-mailed my resume everywhere. Hopefully, I'll get a call from someone."

"My Mom already knows about my job."

"How did that happen?"

"The same way she found out about us. Someone blabbed."

"That's not a bad thing is it?"

"No, but I just like to tell people things myself. Some long distant cousin that I don't know works at the diner that I had lunch in and told my Mom."

"Of course."

"I'm going to rent a U-Haul, one of those big ones and some boxes."

"Good. Get enough boxes for me too."

"Okay."

"Are you excited?" he asks.

"Yeah and nervous too."

"Me too. I'll see you after I get off work."

"Okay."

"Bye, Babe." That's going to take some getting used to.

"Bye, Sammy."

I go to the nearest place that sells boxes. I grab tons of boxes, lots of tape, and huge permanent markers. I want to be packed as much as I can before the end of the week. I can't believe that in one week I will be in L.A. This is so awesome! Maybe I will meet lots of celebrities and plan all of the hit parties. This is going to be so cool!

The cashier with the goofy grin interrupts my thoughts, "That will be $277.95."

"For a bunch of boxes?"

"Well, you also got markers, tape, and our latest label maker."

"I did not pick out a label maker."

"You handed it to me."

"I did?" My shopping is out of control.

He looks at me like I'm the crazy one and says, "Yes."

"Oh, well, I didn't mean to. Sorry. Can you put it back please?"

"No."

"Excuse me?"

"I can't put anything back. Our computer doesn't do that."

"I didn't ask your computer. I asked you." Technology is so not my friend.

"I still can't do it."

"I'm not paying for it."

"You have to pay."

"Look, Mr. Box Guy, I'm not taking the label maker."

"Well, I can't take it back." I don't understand this.

"Well, I'm not taking it or paying for it. That leaves you with one choice. Take it back!!!" I scream. This is ridiculous.

"But I can't take the label maker."

"Ugh! Too much work! Let me talk to the manager."

"I am the manager."

"Are you serious?" This has to be a prank.

"Yes."

"Then take it back!" I stare at him with an evil eye.

"I can't take it back!"

I look at him in total frustration. This is like the twilight zone. Why is this man out to get me? I did nothing to him.

"How about you pay for it, take it outside, and then come back in and get your money back for it?" he asks.

"Are you kidding me?"

"Afraid not."

"Oh, geez!" I swipe my Master Card and put all the boxes and bags in my car. I grab the label maker and go back into the store to get my refund. This is ludicrous!

I hand the label maker back, "Can I have a refund? I don't need this label maker."

"Do you have a receipt?"

I throw my hands up! "You didn't give me a receipt."

He smiles and says, "Then I can't give you a refund."

"This is so stupid! Give me my money!"

"I can't give you a refund without a receipt!"

"You just told me…"

"My policy is stated right above me." I glance up at the big sign that says, "Refunds only with Receet." Oh, geez! He didn't even spell receipt right.

"But you didn't give me a receipt." I say slowly through clenched teeth

"Sorry."

So, I ended up with a very expensive label maker. I can't believe that guy. He totally ripped me off. I think I need some serious fried food to get over this. I hop into my car and speed off to Kentucky Fried Chicken. I need chicken, biscuits, mashed potatoes, and pie.

I pull in through the drive-thru and order everything including pie. I will be totally fine with L.A. as long as they have fast food. I pull up to the window to find my old roommate Kendra, who moved out to live in Africa with her "soul-mate," decked out in a KFC uniform. Her braids were pulled tight into a ponytail. This is going to be so good.

"L.K.? Hey, how's it going?" she asks while handing me my food.

"Great!"

"I see your appetite hasn't changed."

"Nope. I thought you moved to Africa with your "soul-mate" from the Internet."

"That didn't go as planned."

"I see."

"Well, he ended up telling me to meet him in Ohio so that he could tell his family goodbye before we could go. Well, I go to Ohio and find that his address is a prison and he is on trial for murder. He wanted me to help pay his lawyer. His name isn't Mojimbe, it's Jermaine. I totally got scammed."

"Sorry, friend."

"Well, it's totally my fault. Now, I have to work overtime to pay rent on a crappy apartment."

"You can rent our old apartment."

"Are you moving?"

"Yep." I can see the line forming behind me.

"Where?"

"L.A. I got a new job." Horns were honking behind me.

"Here's my number. Please call me later." She hands me a napkin and I take off.

I can't believe that Kendra got scammed. I don't feel very bad about it. She left me in a bind. I do feel bad that her dream guy ended up being a criminal. That sucks, but at least she is back home and maybe taking the apartment. It will be a lot cheaper than getting an ad out.

I scramble up to my apartment with my food, my label maker that I named Bert (He costs enough to have a name), the boxes, tape, and the markers. I guess I should start packing. It's kind of sad. This is my home. I pull open the take-out menu drawer and a tear comes to my eye. I'll never be able to order from these again. I think I'll frame these and put them in my new apartment in L.A.

The phone is ringing. It's probably Mom again telling me what I just bought. We are probably related to that weird box man. I grab the receiver, "Hello."

"L.K., this is Dolly."

"Oh, hey, Dolly! What's up?"

"Mr. Madden said to cancel your U-Haul."

"Why? Am I not moving?"

"Oh, you're moving, but Mr. Madden has paid someone to move all of your things and carry it by plane."

"What about my car?"

"They are taking care of that too. Mr. Madden also said that he will take care of your flight arrangements. He said to just be ready to leave on Thursday at 6:00 a.m."

"Thursday? That's not a week."

"I am just relaying the message, girlfriend."

"Oh, man. Well, I better go so I can find someone to live in my apartment. Bye, Dolly!"

I slam the phone down and call Kendra. She has to live here and she needs to live here by Thursday.

Chapter 22

"L.K.! Girl, get up out of that bed! It is 5:00 a.m. You have to leave in an hour!" Kendra shakes me while she screams.

"Are you kidding? I have only been asleep for two hours and it's your fault."

"I didn't ask you to stay up all night and talk with me," she says flipping her hair.

"Yes, you did."

"Well, maybe I did. I just wanted to have a last sleepover with you. Girl, you are leaving me and I needed to catch up. You have to get up out of my bed."

"I didn't have a choice. I have nothing. Those mover guys took everything I owned yesterday along with my car."

"It feels so good to be here again. I can't believe you are leaving. If you ever come back, you have a place to stay. I'll kick out whoever is living here with me and we'll be roomies again."

"Thanks. Is Sam here yet?"

"Yes, Prince Charming is waiting in the living room."

I can't believe I'm leaving for L.A. It doesn't feel real. I'm going to be living in Los Angeles as the boss at a big party company making lots of money and meeting tons of celebrities. I bet I fall on my face.

I quickly change out of Kendra's pajamas and into my clothes. The only thing I left here was a pair of jeans, a tank top, flip-flops, and my bag. I pull my hair into a ponytail and walk into the kitchen. Sam is sitting there all perfect and clean. I look like a hot mess.

"Hey, Beautiful!" Sam says as he kisses my neck.

"You're kidding, right?"

"No. You are always beautiful to me. Are you ready to go?"

"I guess."

"What's wrong? Aren't you excited to leave? You have your big job and I don't have a job at all."

"That's the thing. I have asked you to change your whole life to move with me. I have everything and you have nothing."

"I have you," he says giving me a sweet kiss.

I push him off me. "Don't be cheesy! You don't even have a job to move for. I think we should just forget about it. I can probably get another job here. I can stay here with Kendra."

"Hey, I like that idea," Kendra chimed in.

"I don't. L.K., you are just scared. We are moving. It will be fine," Sam says as he hands me a cup of coffee.

"I guess I am scared. I'm scared that I'm going to fall on my face. I don't care about the money or the big celebrities. I just want to plan parties. That's fun for me. I just don't want to screw everything up and end up back here with no job."

"You'll be fine. We will be fine, but now we have to go. The Limo's here."

We said our goodbyes to Kendra and Mrs. Tragger. She said she'd kill me if I didn't say goodbye. "Bye Hildie!" I yell at her as we get into the elevator.

"You know I hate that Lora Kate London! Be safe! Call me when you get there and get Sean Connery's digits for me," she yells back.

I sit on my bench carefully. I'm going to miss this bench. It has always been there for me. The bench let me lay on it when I was tired or sad. It put up with me when I was hateful or soaked with rain. I guess this is it. I'm moving to L.A. No more Pete's Pizza or awful Chinese food from across the street. No more Times Square or coffee from Java Joe's. It's like the end of an era.

Sam lifted my head with his hands. "Stop being sad. Our new apartment is going to be great. You won't miss a thing," Sam says as he opens the Limo door for me.

"I guess. I'm just going to miss New York. It's my home."

"I'm going to miss it too."

"Good. We'll have to come back to visit." I hop in the Limo and tell the driver to go.

As we pull into the airport, I realize that we were not going commercial. The side of the jet says, "James Madden." We are going on a private jet! How cool is this! The driver leads us to the jet and helps us get through security.

"I can't believe we are taking a private jet. I feel so fancy," I say as we board the plane.

"Me too. I guess you picked the right boss. Maybe you will have one of these soon."

"Maybe."

The engine starts and we begin to move. This is it! We are flying to L.A. I take out my phone to snap some last minute shots of New York when all of a sudden, we feel a jolt. The pilot walks over to us and takes a seat.

"Aren't you supposed to be flying the plane?" I ask.

"Well, we are having a problem with one of the wheels. We will have to wait a couple of hours before I take you two to L.A. Mr. Madden will be joining us shortly."

"Crap!"

This would only happen to me. I have a fabulous new job in a cool city with lots of celebrities waiting on me and I'm stuck on a runway in a broken plane. We'll probably crash and be stranded on a deserted island with no food and weird animals. Good thing I'm done with my boot. I'd never be able to outrun anything with the boot. Maybe I should get a job at Bloomingdale's. I saw that help wanted poster yesterday.

Sam nudges me, "Hey, you want some peanuts?"

"Sure. Why not? We might need them later on that island."

"What?"

"Never mind. Give me the nuts!" I grab the nuts and slump down into my seat. I just hope we crash on an island with fruit in the trees and not coconuts. I saw how many problems Tom Hanks had with those.

The stewardess walks in front of us and ask, "Would you like to watch a movie while you wait?"

"Do you have Signs?"

Sneak Peak of
From New York to L.A.

Chapter 1

Things cannot get any worse. There is no way that my life can get any worse than it is right now. First of all, we get off that death trap of a plane that rocked, bumped, and basically almost crashed on the way here to this supposedly beautiful city of L.A. that is presently full of smog and rain. I expected to walk off the plane into the sunshine and go to the beach, but nope. It's raining buckets and I'm grateful my honey blonde hair is pulled up into a ponytail. And because of my awesome luck, I was randomly searched by airport security. It really wasn't fair because Sam didn't get searched and he laughed at me the whole time...which didn't help.

By the way, I'm Lora Kate London. Most people call me L.K. I'm originally from New York City, but I'm here in L.A. for my new job as head of a party planning company called Madden Party Company. I was head party planner at Party Central Company, but that got ugly and ended. Word of advice: never date your boss. He will probably sleep with your roommate and fire you.

My new boyfriend and best friend, Sam Bridges, is here with me. He's the tall handsome type with the goofy sandy colored hair, but I love him. I do love him, but not in the "I want to get married right now" kind of love. I'm not into the whole commitment thing right now, but we won't get into that.

Any way, here I am in L.A. standing in front of what was supposed to be the best apartment in the world. The doors have gunshot holes on them. Sam's door looks just like mine. I am looking up to heaven hoping that we are in the wrong place, but then when I look at Sam, I know that we are exactly in the right place.

"What is this? A gang hangout? I thought that you said the apartments were perfect. These are far from perfect. They're scary," I tell him.

"They were affordable," he says cocking his head to one side to read the lovely graffiti. "Does this say what I think it says?"

I shudder. "Probably! Sam, these apartments are awful! I'm not living in this dump. We lived in New York City. Certainly we can afford to live somewhere…nicer."

"You can, but we can't. I had to find two apartments that you could pay for until I find a job. I haven't heard anything from anywhere. The only way that we can live somewhere else is to live together in one apartment. I also know that we would have to get married to do that and you don't want to."

"You say that like you want to get married."

"Well, maybe someday."

"Don't even bring that up right now. I'm not getting married just to live somewhere better than this."

"You don't want to get married?"

"Not anywhere in the near future. Can we not talk about this right now? Let's just go in. The inside may not be as bad as the outside."

"True. Let's go."

I kiss his cheek and we unlock our doors. Yeah, the inside is worse than the outside. Not only is it hideous, it's small. So small, in fact, that the living room, dining room, and bedroom are in the same room. There are three rooms: the kitchen, the bathroom (shower and toilet only), and the living/eating/sleeping room. This is a disaster. Sam must find a job and soon.

I bang on the wall and yell, "Does your place look as crappy as mine?"

"Yes! Are we supposed to eat and sleep in this one room?" he yells back.

"I think so. Just come over here!"

He shuts his door and walks over and wraps his arms around my waist. "I'm so sorry. I didn't realize that these apartments would be this bad. At least we have each other." He kisses me and flips my ponytail.

"Okay. Let's just forget about how bad things are and look at the bright side. We are in Los Angeles. We live where the movie stars live. Well, not exactly in the same area, but definitely in the same city. There is a beach out there waiting for us and Chinese food somewhere. Let's go site seeing."

"Babe, did you forget that it's monsoon season out there?"

"Crap! Well, at least, dinner is waiting for us. James said that he would meet us here in an hour and take us out to eat."

I pull the curtain back from the windows to watch the rain beat down on my already awful day. God has reasons for everything. I must remind myself of that daily. I feel my cell phone buzz in my pocket. I grab my new iPhone that James gave me on the plane, which is like my new favorite toy. I walk outside. "Hello, this is Lora Kate."

"Hey, London, this is James. How are things going so far? Did you make it your apartment okay?"

"Yes and it's a dump!"

"Why are you living in a dump? Your salary is high enough to live somewhere really nice."

"I know, but I have to pay for Sam until he finds a job. Have anything that he can do for pay?"

"Well, you could hire him as your assistant."

"Are you serious? I could do that?"

"You are the boss over here, you know."

"I just thought that I was head planner. I didn't know that I was THE actual boss of everybody. This could be really fun."

"Do you ever listen to me? Now don't get a big head. You still have to plan the major celebrity parties. The office is already filled with staff. They are just waiting on a new boss. I told them you would be there Monday morning. You have the weekend to get settled. You can hire your own assistant and you can fire anyone that is not doing their job."

"Cool! I'm a boss! I never thought that I would be a boss. Does this mean my salary is more than a head planner salary?"

"L.K., did you even read your contract when you signed it? Nevermind. Yes, your salary is more than a head planner makes, but Sam still needs to get a job. He can't live off you."

"I know that and no, I didn't read the contract. I don't have to give you my DNA or anything, do I?"

He laughs, "No."

"I don't know if I want him to be my assistant. I mean, he's great and all, but he's my boyfriend. Then he would also be my employee. Those relationships do not work very well and I should know. What do you think?"

"I think that you can make your own decisions."

"Oh, great! You are no help at all."

"Glad that I could be of service. Don't touch anything. I'll be there shortly to take you out to dinner. I'm sending over some clothes right now."

I put my phone back into my pocket and walk back inside. I look at Sam. He could be my assistant for a while. I give him a big smile.

"What? You are giving me that look that says you want something," Sam says.

"Well, what would you think about being my assistant?" I say smiling.

"Your assistant? Like you would be my boss? I think not!"

"Oh, come on! It would just be until you found another job. You need money and I need to live somewhere I'm not afraid to put my bare feet on the floor."

"Well, I don't know. I don't have any experience with parties."

"All you have to do is answer the phone and bring me coffee. Hey, I like that idea. I officially hire you as my assistant, Mr. Bridges."

"Ugh! What I do for the one I love," he says as he grabs my face and kisses me lightly on my lips.

He pulls me into his chest. I breathe in his cologne and then pull away. "Now, let's get out of this dump before we contact some deadly disease or the Swine Flu…now I don't know what the Swine Flu is, but it sounds gross. I don't like pigs with their wet snouts and their mischievous eyes, so having their flu is not appealing."

Sam gives me a look and shakes his head with a big grin, "I don't think it actually comes from pigs."

"Then why is it called the Swine Flu? Swine are pigs."

"I don't know. Google it."

"Maybe I should pull out my brand new shiny iPhone and check it out?"

"You need an intervention! You are officially addicted to that phone."

"Well, my other phone was stuck in 1999! I needed an update."

He shakes his head. "If we aren't living here, where are we going?"

I wrap my arms around his waist and lean in to smell his cologne again. "We are supposed to wait on James. He said to wait here and not touch anything. I'll need to call the movers later to tell them not to bring our stuff here. He's also having some clothes sent to us before dinner. I'm sure my jeans are not welcome to wherever we are eating dinner."

"I don't mind waiting. I could stand like this all day," he says as he hugs me tighter.

"So could I, but I have a small question," I say as I pull away from his embrace.

"Ask me anything."

"What made you bring up marriage earlier?"

"Of course I think about marriage, L.K. You are my entire life now. Marriage naturally feels like the next step. Don't you love me?"

"Sam, I love you, but we haven't been dating very long. Don't you think it's too soon to talk about it or fight about it in our case?"

"I've loved you for so long now. You've only really loved me for a short time so I guess it does seem a little hasty that I want to be married to you now, but I do want you to know that I feel that way all the time."

"I guess I can kind of see your point. You will just have to be patient with me. I'm not there yet."

"I know. You need to meet my family though. You know that, right?"

"I've already met your family. You took me home with you one Thanksgiving in college."

"You haven't met them as my girlfriend though. Mom really wants to see you again and my brothers and sister too."

Sam's brothers are obnoxious. He has twin brothers, Jonathan and Chord, who are a year younger than him. They are both single and have hit on me on several occasions when they visited New York. His sister, Taylor, is sixteen and has an unnatural obsession with one of those boys from One Direction or used to be One Direction or something.

"I guess we could arrange something this year. Mom and Dad said they could visit at Thanksgiving, so we could go see them at Christmas. It's actually snows where they live in Colorado…Oh, we could go skiing and everything!" That gets me excited. I don't know how to ski, but the clothes are cute.

"That sounds like a plan. They would really like that. You know, a wedding in Colorado at Christmas would be beautiful…"

"I'm sure it would be…" I look at him wondering what in the world he is trying to pull. We just talked about this.

"I'm just kidding. You have to lighten up, London," he says laughing as he pulls me closer to him.

After what seemed a like a year, James finally shows up in a Limo. Sam and I had changed into the nice clothes James sent over and I was grateful that I decided to put my straightener in my carry on. I'm wearing a purple shimmer dress that flares out right above my knees and Sam is wearing a nice charcoal suit. The driver puts our bags in the trunk and we all pile in.

I still can't believe that I'm in Los Angeles! It may be raining now, but it must stop eventually and when it does, I'm going to the beach! I look over at James. He is very tall and apparently growing a beard. He has short, spiky black hair. When I squint, he sort of looks like Matt LeBlanc (Joey from Friends).

"What are squinting at?" James asks.

Blushing, I say, "Nothing."

"Well, let's go to dinner and then I'll put you two in a hotel until you find somewhere to stay," he says.

"Thanks, Mr. Madden. I really appreciate it, Sir," Sam says.

"Sam, please call me James. So, did you accept L.K.'s offer to be her assistant? It has great pay. I mean you can't live off her salary."

Sam's face reddened, "I didn't plan on living off her salary. Moving to L.A. was sort of a quick decision. I didn't have adequate time to get a job. I have my resume at several television stations. I have many options. My degree was in meteorology and television. I can work anywhere. I'm just waiting on some calls."

"Sam, calm down," I say as I take his hand.

"Hey, man, I'm didn't mean anything by that. I just wanted to know if you were going to be her assistant. I will have to get you a contract ready if you are," James says.

"Oh, sorry. Yes, I will be taking the assistant position temporarily."

I smile at Sam. He looks completely embarrassed. He looks at me with those eyes and I melt. He is the sweetest guy in the whole world. For just a minute, I could picture myself wearing a white dress…for just a minute. I shake the feeling away. Sam assumes that I'm chilled and puts his arm around me.

James smiles at me and says, "Well, now that that's settled, let's eat dinner. How does Chateau Marmont sound?"

"I think Chateau Marmont sounds fabulous!" I say in an accent.

The rest of the Limo ride was pretty quiet. James had Sam fill out an application and sign a contract on his laptop. James made reservations for Sam and I to stay in a hotel and I decided to finally read my contract. It's probably best that I read it, right?

As we pull into Chateau Marmont, I soak in the surroundings. This place looks like a castle! Reality hits me. I am in West Hollywood! I could see a celebrity eating dinner! I wonder if there are any Paparazzi hanging around. I wonder if I'll be on the cover of a magazine sitting behind some fabulous celebrity like Beyoncé smiling in the background. I grab Sam's hand and it's so sweaty. He must be excited too.

Everything around me is immaculate…completely out of my comfort zone. I'm used to ramen noodles and chopsticks. I usually eat dinner in my living room wearing my pajamas. I wonder if I'll change. I wonder if I'll start wearing stilettos and sunglasses all the time. That would be pretty weird. I never plan on giving up my Nikes. Comfort is a precious thing.

James goes straight to the hostess as we stand to the side. As they talk, I look at Sam. He looks so out of place and nervous so I give his hand a squeeze and whisper, "It's okay. You can relax."

"This place is super fancy and I'm pretty sure I just saw Chris Hemsworth as we were coming in."

"Really?! I wonder who else is here?"

James motions for us to follow the tall, leggy, blonde hostess to our table. We sit and order our drinks first. The menu is full of amazing food. There are so many yummy choices. I end up choosing the Prime Rib & Twice Baked Black Truffle Potato. Sam orders some sort of Arctic fish and James chooses the Aged Strip Steak Bourguignonne (what the world?).

"So, L.K…" James says.

"So, James…" I retort.

"Are you nervous about starting work? Are you going to be able to handle being a boss?"

"Shouldn't you have asked me that before I signed the contract?"

"You mean the contract you didn't read until an hour ago? Yes, you are probably right, but I have a gut thing. I know you can handle it."

"What if I totally destroy your company?" I say with a mouth full of potato.

"The great thing about a distinguished and settled business is that it pretty much runs itself. My company is full of trained employees with incredible experience. You are very new to this business, but I watched you after your first party. I knew you had raw talent. We just have to get you settled in and introduce you to the company. Everyone is going to love you. Don't worry about the employees. You will hand out assignments, approve things, and plan those big A lister parties."

"What about signing checks, hiring people, dealing with big wigs, and other bossy junk?"

"First of all, I have 10 planners that are great at decision making. You approve major things. You put on the final stamp. If you really don't like someone's idea, then shut it down. Just keep in mind, that I only hire capable people. Everyone who is in their position is there because I know they can do an excellent job. You will meet with the employees to approve their major decisions. You can do that however you like. Sometimes they will just email you or call you. Sometimes you may need to actually need to schedule them to meet you. I will help you get started. I will show you the ropes. Don't fret."

"Well, get ready to have your patience tested."

"I think you have already done that," James laughs.

Sam finally chimes in, "I really appreciate the job, James. Is there anything that I need to know before starting Monday?"

"No kissing in the workplace, answer the phone and emails, get L.K. food or coffee, and don't make the mail people mad."

"Can do, sir."

James nods, "Well, I got you two reservations to stay here in the hotel. They only had one room. Sorry if that makes things complicated."

"If it has a sofa, we can deal," I say.

James pays the check and we begin to leave. I see Cameron Diaz sitting in the corner with a group of people. I cannot stop staring! Cameron Diaz in the same room as me. Today is officially ending better than it began. Would it be completely dorky to ask for a selfie?

Acknowledgements

I just want to say thank you to everyone who has supported me on this crazy and long journey. I can't imagine doing life without all of these people. My first thank you goes to Jesus, my Savior. His grace has set me free and He gave me this gift that you just enjoyed.

Thank you to my husband, Craig, and my sweet daughter, Macy. They are my whole world.

Thank you to my whole family. Ya'll are literally the best. My family is my entire backbone and support system.

Thank you to my friends who continue to encouragement me daily. I'm sure there are more important things to say here, but I'm just grateful for every person who has encouraged me in this process. I couldn't have done it without you. I wish I could list names and not forget anyone, but I know myself well enough to know that I would forget someone. So...you know who you are.

Made in the USA
Middletown, DE
29 December 2018